To David Goodi

"Much of what is wr[...].y
happened. When you
why it was published as a work of. Fiction!."

With best wishes
from:
David Perry.

A Cross by the Wall

A CROSS BY THE WALL

D J Perry

The Book Guild Ltd
Sussex, England

The Book Guild Ltd.
25 High Street,
Lewes, Sussex

First published 1992
© D. J. Perry 1992
Set in Baskerville
Typesetting by APS,
Salisbury, Wiltshire
Printed in Great Britain by
Antony Rowe Ltd.
Chippenham, Wiltshire.

A catalogue record for this book is
available from the British Library

ISBN 0 86332 755 9

*To my son Michael and daughter Sandra —
who came to terms with Germany in their
childhood.*

1

It was such a lovely morning when my sister Angela was married. The peal of the bells at our parish church, St Michael's and All Saints, rang out that day and I can almost hear them now. After the ceremony the ritual of photography began and it seemed endless. It took so long that the officiating chaplain had time to chat to all members of both families joined together that day. When it was my turn he was particularly interested in the fact I was serving in Germany and we discussed conditions in the Federal Republic, economic recovery and, of course, the German people. He asked me about their relationships with the occupying powers in some detail and as he listened to what I had to say there was clearly something else on his mind. It was not long before he came to the point.

'Just to the left of the gate there,' he said pointing. 'That stone wall leads to the resting place of our past parishioners, God rest their souls. At the far end there is one grave that troubles me. No one has ever visited it from Germany to my knowledge. Only one of my flock ever laid flowers there. She used to say that he was some mother's son, and now she is gone poor dear.'

I felt ill at ease as he spoke but knew some kind of response was due.

'Ah yes, the cross by the wall, Padre – it's been there a long time, since September 1940 in fact. Things were very bad here then with Kenley and Croydon so close. You wouldn't expect it to have been otherwise.'

He smiled at this and said things in Germany were a lot worse towards the end of the war.

'Mr Kendrick, your sister tells me you are an RAF pilot. A different generation to those who fought the Battle of Britain of course, but somehow I thought you might be able to help me.

'In what way?' I said guardedly. He smiled again before answering.

'When you return to Germany you might be able to trace some relatives of he who lies beneath that cross by the wall.'

Hoping I did not look as angry as I felt, I replied fairly evenly.

'Well Padre, Germany is still divided as you know. If any relatives are in the GDR there is no way I can trace them. Furthermore, that Luftwaffe war grave is hardly our responsibility. He who lies there did his level best to butcher the lot of us. The Lindsay family, my good friends, are all buried here. For all we know, it could have been his bombs that killed them.'

A look of sadness came over the vicar's face at this.

'Yes, I know how you feel. The Lindsay grave is truly terrible. That young mother and her three sons. You were at school with those boys, I believe?'

Before I had chance to reply we were interrupted by the photographer who wanted the vicar to pose with the bride and groom. That was more or less where matters were left. When Angela and Bill, smothered in confetti, left for the reception, I remember strolling back along that churchyard path towards the covered gates to collect my car. On the way out I glanced to my left at the lone white cross and decided to take a look at it. The paintwork had peeled badly and the wood was beginning to rot. I could hardly make out the once black lettering upon it. Standing there, a flood of memories came back to me – so much had happened since 1940. Suddenly the calls of friends broke into my thoughts. They needed a lift to the hotel. It was time to go.

A few days later, as my leave was coming to an end, my old friends Paul and Heather Channing invited me to dinner. Paul and I had been at school together and our friendship had been a close one ever since. He was a journalist by profession and had spent a number of unhappy years in Fleet Street. When it became obvious he was not destined for further advancement, he accepted a down-market job as editor of our local newspaper. At least the pressure was off him now. Sad of course in some ways, but he seemed more relaxed, was drinking less and his wife Heather not quite as difficult as I had remembered her in earlier years.

Over coffee after the meal I mentioned the chat with the vicar about the war grave and Paul gave me one of his old-fashioned looks.

'Yes, always a mystery that,' he said. 'You and I were barely ten when it happened. So long ago that you've probably forgotten all the rumours flying about those days.'

I had to confess that I had and asked to be reminded.

'Well, if you mean the ones about the Jerry airman,' Paul replied, 'perhaps it would be better if they remained forgotten.'

'Come now,' I said. 'Are you being deliberately mysterious to arouse my interest in the case?'

Paul feigned mock surprise. 'You don't suspect me of being in league with the vicar, surely?'

'I think I know you better than that, Paul – you haven't been near a church since your own wedding!'

Paul pretended to look hurt at this and said he had been to church at least twice since then, when his children were christened.

'I didn't know you were a devout devil-basher, old boy,' he said.

'I'm not, but if we only go to church to be hatched, matched and despatched, it doesn't seem to be a very practical form of support, that's all.'

Paul said something rude at this point and Heather decided to chime in to break the male monopoly. She said that the churches were empty for the same reason the cinemas were – television. That, and the pace of modern life, which meant Sundays were the only days the gardening got done.

'Well,' said Paul. 'That might be true. Getting back to the Blitz and that German war grave, I remember hearing my father telling my mother something when he thought I was out of earshot. Dad was in the LDV in those days before it became the Home Guard. I distinctly heard him say that a German airman who landed by parachute on Plover's Green was lynched by a group of our soldiers. Mum was inclined to dismiss all this as just a bit of wishful thinking on the part of the bloodthirsty elements but Dad stuck to his story. According to Dad, the troops involved had all served with the BEF in France. They remembered the Luftwaffe butchery of French refugees on the roads of Northern France and most of all, the horrors of Dunkirk. There had been an almighty row about the lynching when the police turned up at Plover's. A couple of the soldiers were about to take on the fuzz and would have done, if the LDV from Coulsdon hadn't turned up in strength.'

As I listened to Paul's account there was within me a profound sense of shock.

'Any charges brought by the police?'

'None that I know of. All right, so technically the Jerry was a POW and the Geneva Convention would have protected him. If he *was* murdered then the people of this parish have remained tight-lipped about it ever since, Mike. Our little manor of Tallingwood had a bad war, remember? The 1940 Blitz was bad enough but the flying bombs in '44 were a damn sight worse. This area had the highest percentage of V1 incidents in the UK – with casualty figures to match. No wonder there's a conspiracy of silence about that cross by the wall.'

I knew Paul was right about Tallingwood.

'If what your Dad said about the events at Plover's Green turned out to be true, then you're right about it being better forgotten. Do you think the vicar knows any of this?'

'I doubt it. He wasn't here then. In the Navy, so they say. In any event he's more concerned about relatives in Germany and finding them is going to be a needle in a haystack job, for a start. Having said that, though, this old vicar knows of your interest in military history – your sister Angela blew the gaff on that one and being an intrepid birdman, you might, just might be prepared to do a bit of delving.'

'I can't make out what's written on that cross now,' I said.

'Oh, that's no problem,' said Paul breezily. 'It's all recorded in the church register.'

'Then you are the one to do the delving,' I retorted.

'I'm not the one serving in Germany,' said Paul. 'What's more, you would have access to official war records, combat reports at the Air Ministry and understand all the professional flying mumbo-jumbo relevant to it.'

I smiled at this and called him a devious old bugger – among other things. Heather, by this time had become thoroughly bored and repaired to the kitchen amid a loud clattering of plates. When she had gone I lit a cigarette.

'You, Paul Channing, are undoubtedly on the vicar's side.

All right, who lies there under the cross by the wall?'

'You do understand Mike, that, er, if by some remote chance you ever find any relatives in Germany – not one word of what I've told you can ever be released over there.'

It was my turn to look hurt. 'What do you take me for, Paul?'

He paused before answering. 'You've got a short fuse at times, Mike, and the Germans can be irritating. In the heat of the moment and remembering what happened to the Lindsay family – I just thought ...!'

'Short fuse or not,' I replied. 'Tell me what the church records say.'

Paul produced a slip of paper from within his inside pocket. 'This might be of some help, to begin with.'

It had been typed out and contained just the bare facts. The body interred in grave number 314 at the parish church of St Michael and All Saints, Tallingwood in the county of Surrey was that of Feldwebel K. Neumann who died on 9 September, 1940. He was the occupant of an enemy aircraft which crashed in Vernon Road shortly after 6 pm that day. The Imperial War Graves Commission had erected the cross on 18 September in accordance with the Geneva Convention.

When I had finished reading this I asked Paul, 'How much research have you personally done on this already? If this Luftwaffe sergeant was recovered from his crashed aircraft, how could there be any link with the Plover's Green case?'

Paul raised his hands from the dinner table.

'That's just it. We have to face the possibility that there may have been a cover-up. We seem to be rather good at that sort of thing.'

'Paul, I know there have been a lot of cover-ups of late but isn't there just a chance that you might be letting your newshawk's imagination get the better of you?'

'Yes, of course there's a chance,' he conceded. 'But I have made some enquiries from people who were here at the time. They either clam-up or get nasty.'

I had to admit that such reactions were rather odd and asked Paul to be more specific. This he declined to do.

'See what you can find out in Germany, Mike. There must be some ex-service organisations over there which could help.'

'How little you know about the modern Bundes Replublik' I

11

said. 'World War II is a subject that they all prefer to forget. The younger generation wears the sins of the Fatherland badge under protest and it's mainly the young West Germans of NATO, the new Bundes Luftwaffe at HQ, Allied Tactical Air Forces that I have contact with. I could ask around and see what records are still available.'

Paul seemed satisfied with this and Heather joined us then.

'Come on you two,' she sighed. 'Can't you find something else to talk about – I'm bored!'

This was Heather in one of her more familiar moods. Paul and I changed the subject as bid. By the time Heather had prattled away about her favourite themes – infidelity, hysterectomy, shampoo and set – I began to make a move. The meal was a good one, though, and I thanked them both for a pleasant evening. As Paul stood by the porch to see me out we shook hands.

'Keep in touch, Mike. Good luck and happy landings. I'll let you know if anything else crops up about that war grave case.'

I promised to do the same but secretly felt nothing further could be done. On the way home that night I stopped the car on the edge of Plover's Green. That place where some terrible event could have happened. I thought awhile and tried to make a mental list of all the likely sources that might uncover the mystery. Historical Records Branch, Air Ministry, Bundes Archives, the Red Cross. Imperial War Graves Commission and perhaps the only German I knew who might help. Dieter, a West German Air Force captain, military history buff and, rare for a German – ready at any time to talk about the war. His wife Lotte didn't like him doing this. A good NATO wife. Queen of the cocktail party circuit.

'I shall have to get Dieter on his own for this one,' I thought. 'We'll see.'

2

A week later I was back in harness. The usual backlog had been allowed to accumulate. So much for SASO's leave allocations. For the first few days I was wallowing in NATO Op. orders, phone calls and wishing the group captain would go on leave. By the end of the week I was wilting and, just after 7pm on the Friday I repaired to the mess bar, in need of a jug or two. When I got there, some sort of party seemed to be going on. A bunch of German F104 pilots had made a staff visit that day and my good friend Dieter was much in evidence. As soon as I sidled up to the bar he was upon me.

'Michael! You wicked old bastard. You didn't tell me you were back off leave.'

'No mate – I've been up to my arse in alligators ever since Monday. How's Lotte and the kids?'

'They are all well, Michael, did you have a good leave?'

I said that I had, relating briefly my sister's wedding.

'Oh! Lotte would love to hear about that,' said Dieter. 'She has theories about the British, so lacking in emotion, she wonders how they ever make love at all.'

I fixed what I hoped was a reproving gaze on Dieter. 'Well, you know us better than that, old cock.'

Dieter looked perplexed. 'Old cock – was ist das?'

It was my turn to grin. 'Cockney idiom, Captain Ewalt! Not in the NATO R/T handbook.'

'Hm,' snorted Dieter. 'No more than Berliner Plat Deutsch.'

We both chuckled at this and before long I was drawn into a particularly hectic 'thrash' with the F104 crowd. Towards 9pm I suggested it would be a good idea to sober up. Dieter narrowed his eyes at me.

'Michael – there's something on your mind isn't there? I've felt it ever since you came into the mess. Do you want to talk about it?'

I felt tipsy enough to tell Dieter then what the vicar had told me at Angela's wedding. No mention of anything else. Dieter heard me out, sizing up every word I said. When I had finished he took a deep draught of his Amstel.

'Do you know what aircraft was involved? It's going to be important. A name, a rank, and a date will help, yes, but the Association will need to know more. The Old Comrades are quite active. I might be able to find something. Being so long ago, there may not be many left now, able to help us.'

I tried hard to remember some facts Paul Channing had told me before answering Dieter.

'At present I don't know the aircraft type, although we might be lucky and hear something later.'

Dieter was quick to respond. 'You say the church records state he was the occupant of an enemy aircraft. If it had been a bomber, what of the others in the crew? Would they not be buried with him?'

'Could have baled out,' I said. 'On the other hand, he might have flown alone.'

Dieter wrinkled his nose. 'Yes, he might have been many things. A Feldwebel, you say. Many of the Luftwaffe pilots were NCOs, then again ... Leave it with me Michael, I'll see what I can do. Incidentally, don't mention any of this to Lotte – you know how she is about the war.'

I promised not to and we both left the bar as the singing started. The F104 crowd were beginning to get warmed up.

By pure coincidence, Paul Channing's letter arrived the next day. This is what it contained:

'There wasn't an awful lot left of Neumann's plane. Another friend of mine remembered the incident vaguely and said the only recognisable pieces were the twin rudders. This pins it down to either a Dornier bomber or a Messerschmitt 110. Either way, what happened to the others, if it was a Dornier or the wireless operator-air gunner, if it was a 110? I spoke to Mrs Maynard who still lives in Vernon Road and although only a child of seven at the time, she remembered quite a lot. She said the plane 'shrieked' on its way down and she and her brother were very frightened down in the garden shelter. When the plane struck the ground, the force of it was like a bomb. It crashed into some elm trees, initially, which lined the bottom of

14

their neighbour's garden. Unfortunately, the neighbours were elderly then and are no longer living. They would have been interesting to talk to! One other piece of information came from the milkman. He was a kid like us in those days. He said he saw the plane in its death plunge. It was in a vertical dive and by the noise it was making, under full power. I of course asked him to describe the aircraft. All he could remember was it had twin engines.'

Back to the bomber/fighter dilemma again.

I folded Paul's letter and rang Dieter's number. Dieter wasn't there – had to go to Fassburg on a staff visit, I was told. I asked them to get Dieter to ring me on his return.

That evening, the wives' club were holding one of their bring and buy sales in the mess. Lotte Ewalt, Dieter's wife, stood chatting with a group of ladies and, catching my eye, waved vigorously. I felt I should wait and sure enough, Lotte detached herself from the rest of the 'hens'. Giving me one of her dazzling Marlene Dietrich smiles – for to Marlene Dietrich she bore a certain resemblance, she opened up with full armament.

'Michael Kendrick – where have you been? Very naughty! You haven't told me a thing about your sister's wedding.'

This I rectified on the spot and offered to buy her a drink. She declined and listened intently to my account of Angela's nuptials. Always a good listener, our Lotte! I asked when Dieter was due back and she frowned.

'Oh, Lord knows! He's had to go up to Fassburg again. There's been another F104 crash. Damned things. Why don't they get rid of them?'

I replied as tactfully as I could. 'The aircraft is OK, Lotte. Other NATO Air Forces are using them. Dieter's an expert after two tours, you know. If anyone can sort out the problems he can.'

'Oh! you men!' she huffed. 'Loyalty to the last! When are you coming to dinner, Michael?'

'Well Lotte dear, let's get der alter Mann back from Fassburg first and I'll be delighted – any time, you know that.'

She then fixed me with what I can only describe as a penetrating gaze.

'There is a letter for Dieter, it arrived this morning. It bears the Luftwaffe Old Comrades Association postmark on the reverse of the envelope. You know how deeply I feel about resurrecting the past, Michael. Perhaps you can help me when Dieter gets back. When I get it out of him – exactly what the letter is about – and I will, you could be invaluable, is it?'

'Yes Lotte – invaluable. You've been studying again, bravo Madam!'

'All right Michael' she sighed. 'I'll get Dieter to ring you. By the way, how is your love life? Any amorous adventures on leave?'

I grinned at this. 'Well, you know us Brits, Lotte – pretty cold-blooded lot!'

Giving me a sideways glance, Lotte smiled. 'Still playing the field, then!'

'I've got to hand it to you, Lotte – your idiomatic English is brilliant!'

A group captain's wife suddenly descended upon us.

'Lotte dear, we need you desperately,' she announced.

I felt rescued. This group captain's lady I didn't care for and I was barely acknowledged. Lotte said she would be in touch and I went into dinner. As I sat at table trying to do justice to a German version of 'toad-in-dem-hole' I thought about that letter waiting for poor Dieter. It was pretty obvious that he had been 'sniffing' on my behalf and when Lotte found out, she would eat me for breakfast!

The rest of the week was punctuated by SASO behaving like Caligula and our own group captain, singularly devoid of ideas, brain picking his staff without shame.

On Thursday the phone rang.

'Michael! it's Dieter.'

Swallowing hard I did my best to sound breezy. 'Oh hello mate, had a good time with the birds of Fassburg then?'

'Too busy for that sort of nonsense – look – as Glen, our Yank would say – the spaghetti's in the fan.'

'In what way Dieter?'

'I think I've found your man. Trouble is, Lotte knows about it.'

'Oh God, I knew she was on to something when I met her in the mess earlier in the week.'

'Yes, she told me about it. She's after your blood as well as mine! I've tried to explain things to her. The bit about reconciliation. Can you come over on Saturday and – well,

16

give me a hand?'

'I'd better wear my flak jacket. All right. What time?'

'Make it about 8 pm.'

'OK. Any joy at Fassburg?'

'Could be servicing – we're not paying enough for skilled technicians in the Bundes Luftwaffe. Pay peanuts – get monkey's etc.'

'Yeah. OK Dieter, see you Saturday.'

When I put the phone down on its cradle I couldn't help feeling very worried indeed. As if the F104 crashes weren't bad enough, now there was going to be unpleasantness with Lotte.

It was with considerable relief on Saturday that on arrival at the Ewalt's married quarter, I wasn't the only guest. Lotte had invited Glen and Jo Hudson, an American couple on an exchange tour from USAF. I liked Glen and his wife was full of fun. Lotte produced one of her glittering meals and Jo Anne had us all in stitches with the latest Rheindahlen scandals. Time passed quickly and before I knew what had happened the Hudsons were preparing to leave. Jo Anne claimed that her baby-sitter's cab turned into a pumpkin at midnight and thanked the Ewalts for a great evening – which it was. I made a move too but Lotte was much too quick for me.

'Come on Michael, you've no work tomorrow. No need to rush off.'

I knew darned well what that meant. She was just waiting to get Dieter and I alone. When the Hudsons had left Lotte came back to the lounge.

'Have a nightcap Michael, you look tired. Been working too hard, I shouldn't wonder. Dieter Liebchen, get Michael an Asbach brandy, I know it's a favourite of his.'

Dieter duly obliged and I noticed he took a generous glass for himself. 'Shades of things to come,' I thought. Lotte sat herself down on the settee and eyed us both with a look that spoke volumes.

'Michael, I know I've said this before but we Germans have a difficult time here. We are trying to be accepted as a nation of civilised human beings, particularly those of us in the military. How are we to do this if the war is constantly dug up and aired as a conversation piece?'

Dieter wasn't going to let his wife get away with that.

'Lotte, Liebling, it's not like that, we don't dig up anything constantly. Only very occasionally and I like to think we face up to things honestly and squarely.'

It was my turn to say something and I said it.

'Lotte dear. I'm very fond of you and Dieter, not to mention those two young scalliwags of yours tucked up safely in bed. Fact of the matter is, I think something can be done to heal the wounds of war. Dieter must have told you what happened at Angela's wedding.'

'Yes he did and I'm not at all sure that any useful purpose would be served by it.' Lotte was bristling.

'Do you think it's right that the location of this Luftwaffe war grave should remain unknown to any relatives in Germany?' asked Dieter.

Lotte was adamant. 'They, if they're still living – have had plenty of time to enquire. The fact that no one has come forward after all these years shows clearly the matter is, like Feldwebel Neumann, at rest and should be left so.'

Dieter was going to say something to Lotte then and I could tell he was annoyed. I butted in, just in time.

'This vicar of ours in Surrey is a good Christian, Lotte. He wants to find Neumann's relatives if he can. When he's found them, perhaps he will feel a modest beginning has been made. A beginning to forgiveness, reconciliation and the acceptance of which you speak. I had no one other than Dieter to turn to. If anyone is to blame here it's me, Lotte. I'm the one who's been doing the digging but I honestly thought it was in a good cause. We don't have to publicise things. The whole matter can be dealt with discreetly. If only you, Dieter, and I know about it – what harm can be done?'

Lotte seemed a little hesitant.

'It's the press, Michael. I personally don't think you will find any relatives now but, should you find them? Oh yes! A great human interest story could be splashed across the front pages! Just think what *Der Spiegel* and your *Daily Express* could do with that.'

'That would depend entirely upon the relatives' said Dieter. 'We would need to guard against that sort of thing, of course!'

Lotte was still unmoved. 'No boys – it's not right. Oh Michael, I judged you too harshly! What is it you say in English – "The road to Hell – being paved . . . ?".'

I finished the sentence for her. Lotte suddenly stood up and I took this as my cue to take my leave. At the front door Dieter gave me a conspirator's wink. Lotte put a hand to my cheek.

'I'll think about all this, Michael. In the meantime, I suppose Dieter ought to tell you what he's been able to find out, so far. "Schlafen Sie gut, Herr Hauptmann."'

Dieter grinned. 'I'll pop over to your office on Monday, Michael, schlafen Sie gut indeed, "old cock" – immer ganz allein.'

3

On the Monday, after I got back to the office when SASO's 'prayer' meeting was over at 10 am, Dieter was sitting at my desk reading that month's issue of *Flight*. I put the kettle on for some coffee as Dieter opened his brief-case to take out some papers.

'Well, Michael, a little information for you. The Old Comrades don't seem to have anything yet but they were good enough to contact the Rot Kreuz. It seems that in the summer of 1940 Herman Goering had let it be known that as the Wehrmacht would be occupying England within six weeks, there was not a detailed requirement for them – the Red Cross in Sweden – to do much on the Luftwaffe's behalf! My own view is that Goering did not want the true losses during the Battle of Britain to be generally known. However, at the end of the war the German people were beginning to ask a lot of questions. Through various pressure groups, the German and Swedish Red Cross authorities were able to get in touch with your Imperial War Graves Commission. By that time, there were many more RAF graves in Germany than there were Luftwaffe ones in England. It was agreed that a proper maintenance programme should be drawn up and the graves cared for. You can imagine the haggling that went on about the cost of it all!'

I said I could imagine it.

'Everybody was broke at the end of the war, and if our Treasury had anything to do with it, the IWGC would be lucky to squeeze more than a bob or two out of them.'

Dieter offered me a cigarette and continued.

'By 1946 we started to collect the records supplied to us and we in turn made a modest start on the much bigger job to be done here. From the alphabetical lists held by the Red Cross, we were able to come up with this: Kurt Neumann, born in

20

Salmisch, Bavaria in 1916, was listed as missing on 9 September, 1940. According to British records, Neumann was killed on that date and buried in the nearest Anglican church to the crash site.'

I had started to make some notes as Dieter spoke and interrupted him at this point.

'Did they name the place of burial?'

'Yes they did,' said Dieter frowning. 'They passed it on to the Soldaten Friedhof people, that's our own War Graves Commission, in the hope that relatives might be traced. Being six years after the event and remembering the state of chaos here in Germany, many enquiries went unanswered. This seems to have been the case here. In this morning's post I received a letter. It's from the general secretary of the Bundes Luftwafff archives in Bonn. It advises me to contact a certain Hugo Bennecker, a garage proprietor of 9 Hohestrasse, Koblenz. Before coming here, Michael, I rang Bennecker. He's prepared to meet us. He said he knew Kurt Neumann well. They were both trained at the Fighter School, Werneuchen, near Berlin in the spring of 1940. On graduating, they were posted to ZGII as replacement pilots in the July of that year. He didn't want to say any more than that.'

I was delighted to hear all this and said so.

'Dieter, you are an absolute gem!'

'Count not your chickens!' grinned Dieter. 'This old Bennecker might be genuine. On the other hand he might not be. A lot of wierdos around, you know!'

I thought about this and realised Dieter, as usual, was quite right to sound a note of caution.

'Certainly no harm in nipping down to Koblenz for a noggin or two to find out. Think we could manage it?'

Dieter smiled broadly. 'Might be able to fix it, if Lotte doesn't read the Riot Act.'

We giggled like a couple of schoolboys at that. My phone rang. It was business most urgent. Dieter got up to leave. I asked my caller to hold for a second, putting my hand over the mouthpiece, and turned to Dieter as he made for the door.

'I'll listen out for you on all channels, mate. Let me know what you decide.'

Dieter nodded.

'Sure thing, Michael. Could be next weekend. Suit you?'

21

I said it would, adding 'My love to Die Königen.'

Dieter giggled again.

'Yes, she would like that. Queen Charlotte of Rheindahlen – must tell her that. Wiedersehen, old cock.'

'Oh Lord,' I thought. 'More flak from Lotte – I'll be bound.'

It was all arranged by Wednesday. Dieter and I would drive down to Koblenz on Saturday afternoon. When I asked about Lotte's reaction Dieter cleared his throat.

'Know what she said? "You are going to do this stupid thing, Dieter Ewalt, whether I approve or not, go then and play your silly war games. Much good it will do you and the rest of us!" Hot tongue and cold shoulder for supper that night, I can tell you!'

On the Saturday, we took the autobahn route south of Cologne to Koblenz. It was a nice run and Dieter's Taunus purred along happily. I began to think about things on the way down and put it to Dieter squarely.

'How on earth did Archives put you on to this old buzzard in Koblenz? The Red Cross had little to tell us. Somebody must have tipped them off at Bonn.'

Dieter tapped his fingers on the steering wheel.

'We have a passion for statistics, Michael, records feed the German soul. We like to be regarded by the rest of you as efficient, you know. Maybe, somebody thought no harm would come of this.'

I couldn't help asking Dieter then, 'How about you, old friend? Any strong feelings?'

'None Michael', he replied, 'if you are worried about Lotte and I, fear not. She will get over it. I see all this as an interesting piece of military history. Just like you do. Fascinating in fact. Anyway, let's wait and see when we get to this old buzzard as you call him.'

Feeling a little guilty at what I had called Bennecker I offered Dieter a polo mint, which he declined.

'He was lucky to survive the war. Pre-war Luftwaffe trained and through the Battle of Britain. What do you think happened?' I asked.

'Yes, I've been thinking that myself,' said Dieter. 'There's no way he could have survived the full onslaught of air operations after 1940. Must have been a POW either in your country or the Soviet Union. If it was the latter, he will be interesting for us of NATO to talk to, don't you think Michael?'

I had to smile at that. 'Good old Dieter,' I thought to myself. 'Practical to the last. Is he one step ahead of me on this one already?' Suddenly, another thought came to mind.

'Well at least the aircraft type has been resolved, Dieter. ZG stood for Zerstoerer Gruppe, didn't it?'

Dieter nodded.

'That's right, Messerschmitt 110. You're probably thinking the same as me. What of the Bortshutzer/air gunner? Perhaps Bennecker can throw some light upon that too!'

When we arrived at Koblenz the town was busy. Lot of traffic about. Dieter managed to edge into the Hohestrasse and was quick to spot the garage, emblazoned with the name of Bennecker. As we drove into the forecourt, there were several near-new Mercedes for sale in the showroom and Dieter chuckled.

'Well, he seems to be running a prosperous little business. No nut-case, this one!'

We parked the Taunus and went into Reception. A young woman was on the phone and we waited for her to finish the call. Dieter introduced himself and said Bennecker was expecting us. 'Bright young thing,' pressed a buzzer and after some rapid exchanges with a male voice on the other end of the line, asked us to be seated. We didn't have long to wait. A short balding man with the beginnings of a weight problem suddenly appeared at the side door. He smiled, we shook hands and, to my relief, he spoke English fluently, albeit with a transatlantic accent. He seemed vaguely amused by us. A half smile was never far away and his deep set blue eyes scrutinised us both as he spoke.

'My flat is upstairs gentlemen, follow me please.'

This we did and after mounting a thick carpeted staircase entered a tastefully furnished lounge. Bennecker was a good host. We were offered a wide choice of drinks and after the usual pleasantries, we sat down and began to discuss the reason for our visit. Bennecker explained that a retired Luftwaffe general had been in touch from Bonn and had reminded Bennecker of his early days with ZGII. The general had been a major then and had gone right through the war without a scratch.

Dieter muttered.

'Must have been one of the Experten!'

Bennecker confirmed this but added quickly that the general preferred to remain anonymous.

'Gentlemen, it is really about Kurt Neumann that you have come here. So long ago now. It was perhaps an unusual friendship between us. Bavarians and Rhinelanders don't often mix too well, you know. I think the fact we were both Catholics started our friendship. We took communion together at the base chapel of Werneuchen. Later of course, operating out of Crécy in France, our devotions were conducted from the padre's tent.

'Kurt was a year younger than I. His father was the postmaster of Salmisch in Bavaria. His mother had died suddenly in 1938 – the year both Kurt and I were accepted for pilot training. There were two sisters I believe. One younger than Kurt. I can't remember their names now. Anyway, things started to happen in the West that summer of '40 as you know. It was the beginning of August by the time Kurt and I were sent to France. The Zerstoerer Gruppen had sustained losses and we were the first batch of replacements. We did several combat missions as soon as we arrived. Portland, Southampton, Thorney Island. All lively missions. I lost an engine at Thorney Island and nearly ditched in the Channel. Kurt had to nurse his Zerstoerer back from Portland with a rear fuselage looking like a sieve. The gunner died and Kurt was – well, you can imagine. Blamed himself, I think. Lacking experience, he felt his combat tactics against the British fighters could have been better.

'There was not a lot of time for Kurt to brood on this. The Gruppe was led by a fire-eater and we were entering a new phase of the battle by September. Seelöwe invasion plan was well advanced. The fighter defences had been weakened in England and we were told that the week 7–15 September was going to be it. Goering himself came out to see us. All lined up we were with the "fat one" telling us that the RAF was on its knees. I recall exchanging glances with Kurt at that one. Thinking about Portland and Thorney Island, there wasn't much sign of weakness there.

'Anyhow, the attacks on London began that weekend. Saturday 7 and again 8 September. The British were expecting us to go for their airfields again. We caught London by surprise and set the East End and Dockland ablaze. The fighters met us on the way home over Kent and a running battle carried on over the Channel. Although the Zerstoerer was not as agile as the defenders, its forward firing armament of cannon and machine gun was formidable. Both Kurt and I got a Hurricane each. They just blew up. No parachutes. We were given a rest on the 8th. Other ZGs did that day's work. By this time, both Kurt and I had new gunners, mine was a lad from Kassel – just twenty. Willi Schroeder. Kurt had a tall gangling boy from Munich which pleased him. Felt secure, I suppose, with a fellow Bavarian to protect his backside! This "Junger" was experienced. Had done more missions than Kurt. Been with the Gruppe since the beginning of the war. Rudi Baumbach by name and holder of an Iron Cross. Quite a shrewd choice, this, at staff level. Somebody must have felt Kurt needed a boost after his Portland scare. As we weren't flying on that Sunday, Kurt and I attended mass and communion. On the way back to the tent we talked about Goering's visit and the way things were going. Kurt said we had to face up to the fact that the RAF was the first well trained and modern air force we had come up against. I pointed out that the numerical superiority of the Luftwaffe was bound to bleed them to death in the end. We chewed this over for some time. I remember Kurt saying at one point that his father had been an infantry sergeant in the First World War. Had fought the British for three years and had a sneaking respect for them. Said the British were too much like us. Blood ties, history and all that. Kurt seemed quiet for the rest of that day. Maybe he had a premonition. We knew another mission was to be mounted the next day and in the morning of the 9th, a Monday, we were all briefed for London again.

'Our secondary target was the Vickers factory at Wey-bridge, Surrey. Our job was to provide top cover for the Dorniers to rendezvous with us over Cap Gris Nez in the late afternoon. Our Gruppe put up thirty Zerstoeren that day. Kurt and I flew as wing men to flight leaders, stepped up in layers from about 6000 metres altitude. We joined up with the Dorniers over the Channel. Some of their Kampfgruppen were running late. Quite a lot of cumulus about which made formation keeping difficult. As we drew near to Dungeness the cloud thinned out. Visibility was good then and I remember Willi, my gunner, saying it looked "quiet". I said it was too quiet and wondered where the RAF was. Willi reckoned the Tommies were going to wait and see where we were really heading, before letting their bulldogs loose. He turned out to be right. There was still no reception committee, even at the borders of Surrey. Over on our right we began to see the vast built-up areas of London. Still no defending fighters. At this point, I began to suspect that Goering might have been right. Suddenly – all hell was unleashed. My flight leader's Zerstoerer seemed to be covered in a shower of sparks and it veered away from me to the left with smoke pouring from both engines. I felt a severe jolt and the glass of my flight instruments splintered in all directions. Then we saw them. Dozens of Hurricanes overtaking us now they had caught us so completely unawares. Remembering the usual drill, I opened up to full power and started to turn away in case any more Hurricanes were behind us. It was then that I caught sight of Kurt and his flight leader. They were doing the same as me. Kurt's leader told us to close up. That meant a defensive circle again. All right if you could out-turn the Tommies, which we seldom could. At least we had speed and our leader took us into a shallow dive. The Dorniers below us were under attack now. One of them was ablaze already. Leader was obviously planning to give the Dorniers some help and took Kurt and I down to their level. I couldn't believe my eyes as we neared our own bombers. The sky seemed full of Hurricanes. "Where the hell have they come from?" I thought.

'We were to learn later, of course, that these were all from 12 Group, the first of the Big Wing attacks, normally held in reserve for the defences north of London. We must have been somewhere east of Croydon when this happened. I saw two Hurricanes collide trying to get at the same Dornier! Only one parachute. At least our leader had got us among the Hurricanes and I took several deflection shots as they swam into gunsight view. Then I saw it. Kurt's Zerstoerer suddenly reared up and rolled onto its back. As this happened, Flight Leader banked sharply to starboard and I heard him shout on R/T to "Break, scatter". The Hurricane responsible for Kurt's unusual manoeuvre suddenly dived below us, missing Leader by a few feet. I was determined to get that Tommy and although

Willi – my gunner – was now firing his gun and yelling, I went after that Hurricane. He knew he was being followed. Could see me in his mirror. Twisting, turning, yawing all the time, making my aiming problem difficult. Yes, he knew what he was doing – that one! Willi was getting hysterical by now.

'"Damn it, Mensch, we've got two Spitfires behind us! Dive, break dive for the love of God!"

'So I did just that! I pushed my Zerstoerer to the limits and nearly hit a Dornier in the process. The pursuing Spitfires obviously thought the Dornier was bigger fish and broke off their attacks upon me to attend to it. By the time I pulled out of that dive, I was sweating like a pig and flying just above some roof tops. I had no idea where I was. The stand-by compass still seemed to be working and glancing at the sun, I had at least some sense of direction and kept going south. Sooner or later I'd cross the coast and get a fix, hopefully before the RAF had other ideas. Luck was with me. I crossed the coast between Worthing and Littlehampton; I remembered this from my earlier mission to Thorney Island. I stayed low and asked Willi how he was.'

'"I'm sorry, Feldwebel Bennecker, I shouldn't have called you Mensch," was all he said.

'It must have been nervous reaction I suppose but I started to laugh. Willi joined in and we laughed until the tears of relief came.

'Well, I got back to Crécy. I was the only one of our "schwarm" of four. Both leaders and Kurt were missing. I told our intelligence officer everything I had seen. He gave me a stiff cognac and I flopped onto my cot in the tent. I kept seeing Kurt rolling over on his back after that crazy climb. That stunt wasn't in the tactics manual. I was convinced he had been hit.'

At this point, Bennecker said he hoped he was not boring us and offered to refill our glasses.

'On the contrary, Herr Bennecker' I said, 'please go on.'

Dieter declined a recharge of his glass as he would be driving but, like me, wanted to hear the rest of Bennecker's story.

'Well, I got mine on 15 September', he said with a smile. 'As things were at the time, it was inevitable, wasn't it? They gave me the Iron Cross on the 14th – what a laugh! I don't think the British bobby who arrested me was all that impressed by my decoration. I had to bale out over Romney Marsh in Kent.

27

Poor Willi Schroeder never made it. He was riddled by the time I climbed over the side. I spent the first few months of my captivity in London and Cumberland. In 1941 they sent us to Canada. I stayed the whole war there. Didn't get back here to Germany until 1946.'

Bennecker had gone to the trouble of preparing a cold buffet for us and very good it was too. As we sat at his oak table to enjoy it, Dieter was the first to put some questions.

'Did you ever get a chance to contact any of Neumann's relatives?'

'I started to write a letter to his father in Bavaria a few days after Kurt was shot down. I never finished it, never had the chance to.'

'You had no idea what happened to Baumbach, the gunner?'

'None at all. If he managed to bale out and survive, we would have met up in captivity.'

Dieter looked at me as if to say, 'Go on – it's your turn.' I nodded and then asked Bennecker a question.

'I take it from what you said that you were too busy fighting for your life to have time to spot any parachutes coming from Neumann's aircraft?'

'That's right. Too busy indeed. Quite frankly, Herr Kendrick, it's my belief that Kurt was unconscious or even dead long before he hit the ground. That Zerstoerer was under full power when it rolled over. That would have meant a spiral dive with so much G-force, nobody could have got out of it.'

We spent the next half hour chatting about Dieter's flying experience, which interested Bennecker. He asked me about my tours on Hunters and said he often wished he'd had the chance to fly jets.

'You must forgive me if I seemed a little amused when you arrived,' said Bennecker with a smile. 'Here you were – two pilots, one German – one British – comrades, colleagues in NATO. Come all this way to see me. Some irony in all that I think!'

We thanked him for his help and he promised to keep in touch with Dieter, just in case he heard anything more from the general in Bonn. I left an open invitation for him to call in at the mess in Rheindahlen should business ever bring him that way. We exchanged phone numbers, shook hands and rose to leave.

As we climbed into the Taunus in the forecourt, there was a rapid exchange in German between Bennecker and Dieter. Something about thirty Reichmarks and a Mercedes. Whatever it was, it amused Dieter no end.

As we edged our way out of the Hohestrasse to rejoin the autobahn. I asked Dieter what Bennecker had said that was so funny.

Dieter chuckled again. 'A free translation would be: "If you ever catch up with that bugger Baumbach, remind him he owes me thirty Reichmarks. With the interest accrued over the years, I could afford another Mercedes for the showroom!"'

I thought this was a fairly typical example of aircrew humour, if a little macabre. How alike all flying men were, irrespective of nationality! Dieter wanted to know what I thought of Bennecker.

'Well, everything he told us rang true. It was an honest account of that phase of the war. On detail, I couldn't fault him anywhere.'

Dieter swerved to avoid a cyclist.

'His memory was damn good. Then again, I suppose having lived through all that, it must have left a scar on his soul. One of the first things I will do is get in touch with the Bundes Post. See if we can find out anything about Neumann senior. Whether he still lives or not or where.'

I thanked Dieter for this and said I could at least start writing to a chum of mine in England now.

Dieter turned the 'Blaupunkt' radio on to catch the news, as we joined the autobahn. We listened to the bulletin together and I understood enough to know the Russians were attempting to ship nuclear-armed missiles to Cuba. Dieter's reaction was cool.

'So, the first move in the game of chess – perhaps. This nice looking young American president is now to be tested. We'd better call in at HQ before going home, Michael.'

I nodded and Dieter stepped on it. We arrived at Rheindahlen just before 7 pm. When we saw the notice 'State Red' at the main gate, Dieter swore. With a screech of brakes we arrived at the HQ car park. As I climbed out of the Taunus Dieter said, 'See you on the field of battle – old cock.'

When he said that, I felt that what he and I had listened to in Koblenz was about as relevant as the Battle of Hastings. I didn't get out of the command bunker for three days.

4

It was during the crisis which brought the world to the brink of annihilation that Paul Channing began to receive the first of his threatening letters. Some were more threatening than others, all anonymous of course. With all the questions that Paul had put to so many people in Tallingwood about the Plover's Green affair, it must have been a topic of conversation manor-wide. One morning, as Paul was re-drafting the adverts column, the vicar of St Michael's rang him.

'Hello Paul, it's John Latimer. Would it be possible to call in to see you one day in the week?'

Paul glanced quickly at his desk diary.

'Oh, hello Vicar, yes I think so. What about this afternoon? Say about three.'

Latimer said that would be convenient. Paul opened one of his desk drawers and took out an envelope bearing a BFPO post mark.

'By the way, I've got a letter here from Michael Kendrick, our intrepid birdman in Germany. Seems he has some information for us.'

There was a long pause before the vicar responded.

'Ah yes, well, it's about that I want to see you. Three o'clock then – thank you.'

Paul thought the Reverend John sounded a bit tense. 'Now what', said Paul aloud and his secretary, Miss Watkins, peered over the top of her spectacles.

'Mr Channing, you won't forget the amateur dramatic club coverage at four will you?'

Paul assured her he wouldn't and suggested she took an early lunch.

At five past three the vicar duly appeared in Paul's office, glancing uneasily at the formidable Miss Watkins. Paul had told Millie Watkins the vicar's business was likely to be of a private nature. She sniffed, picked up some papers and as a parting shot said she would be in the printing room if she was wanted. The vicar looked relieved and took the chair that was offered him. When 'La Watkins' closed the door, rather firmly Paul thought, he smiled and invited the vicar to open the proceedings.

'Paul, I'll come straight to the point. I'm very grateful to you for taking an interest in our war grave but I have heard certain views expressed which — well, worry me!'

Paul nodded.

'Yes, I expect you have. Anything unpleasant?'

The vicar frowned.

'No, not really. Why do you ask that?'

Paul thought for a moment.

'Tell me about your views first, Vicar.'

'It was at our last parish council meeting. I was told that there were still many in Tallingwood who did not necessarily share my hopes of tracing any relatives in Germany. They said it was still too soon for that. We had a long discussion about this and I'm happy to say I found one ally, at least, a British Legion man, ex POW. You probably know him, Albert Squires?'

Paul said he did know Squires but not all that well.

The vicar continued.

'Albert likes his pint. Apart from the Legion Club he seems to be a regular customer at the Red Lion. At a darts match there one evening he overheard a conversation about you and some of the enquiries made recently. Without naming anyone he said that certain "lads" thought you should be careful. There were some around in Tallingwood who did not take kindly to Kraut lovers, as he put it. We live in a violent world, Paul. So much of it can be laid at the door of excessive drinking, I'm afraid. Rather than have anything like that happen perhaps we should reconsider things.'

Paul took a deep breath.

'Well, Vicar, it's up to you of course, but don't you think all this was just the beer talking?'

'It's possible, yes, and we do seem to get an awful lot of war films on the telly. Young people today must be influenced by them. However, I thought it only fair to tell you about the council's meeting though.'

'Yes, thank you, Vicar. You might as well know what facts have come out of Germany since this case was opened. I have heard from Flight Lieutenant Kendrick by the way.'

The vicar brightened up at this.

'How good of him. I didn't think he was all that keen to help us.'

'No he wasn't, but his interest in history probably got the better of him. Anyway Mike was lucky. Got a lot of cooperation from our former enemies. Although not tracing any relatives as yet, he's got a lot of personal information about the deceased. One of the facts coming out of all this which might be relevant is that Neumann was a devout Roman Catholic. If his family knew he was buried in an Anglican church they might have held strong views about it. Do Catholics consider a Protestant church to be "hallowed ground", Vicar?'

'Oh, I don't know. Some might feel it's not. It depends on individuals. The fact he was given a Christian burial in a time of great peril to this country should convince even the staunchest RC that what was done, was well, how shall I put it – the decent thing?'

Paul leaned back in his chair.

'Precisely – my views entirely. We won't really know if the religious differences are at the root of this until we find Neumann's relatives. Mike's got a lead. Only a faint one. Miles away from the Rhineland. Right down in southern Bavaria. It could be quite a time before he gets the chance to follow it up. In the meantime I'm going to put the clamps on any further enquiries. Stop people from talking about it at least!'

'Yes, very wise I think. Young Kendrick's done well to find out as much as he has. For my part, I'll play things down too. By the way, did you know there are plans to re-inter German war dead in Staffordshire?'

Paul said he didn't and asked the vicar for details.

'The state of the graves in this country is a matter of concern to those relatives who have visited them. There are so many of them in churchyards in southern England. Financial restrictions make the upkeep very difficult. The West German Government is raising the money for the work to be done. It will take some years to complete and our war grave is due to be moved next summer. The final resting place will be at Cannock Chase. It will have inter-denominational status. An ideal solution, I feel.'

Paul thanked the vicar and said he would write and tell Kendrick all about it. Thus the interview ended. Paul saw the vicar to the door. Millie Watkins watched the departure and gave another sniff of disapproval.

When Paul got back to his desk the phone was ringing. It was his wife, Heather.

'Do you want me to take that dreadful dinner jacket of yours to the dry cleaners? Paul, I asked you to do something about it last week.'

Paul reached for his cigarettes.

'What's the panic? It's not that bad!'

Heather disagreed.

'We are supposed to be attending the Country Club dinner this Saturday – in case you've forgotten!'

Paul had forgotten.

'OK, take it to Dunmores, not those thieves at Braddocks. Have you paid the club for the tickets?'

There was a heavy sigh from Heather.

'You were supposed to have done that last week, Paul. Do I have to do everything? You'd better get over there this evening and settle with them, otherwise we shall be the laughing stock of Tallingwood; not as if that would be anything new!'

Paul was about to say something extremely coarse and rude but thought better of it.

'All right Heather. Sorry and all that but I have been busy.'

His wife's response was fairly predictable.

'You think I haven't been busy? We don't get out nearly enough. When we do get the chance, you make a Horlicks of it!'

Millie Watkins suddenly appeared at Paul's office door. She pointed to her wrist watch as a reminder of his next appointment.

'OK, Heather. Got to rush off now,' said Paul. 'I'll sort it all out and I'll be home about seven. Don't worry about supper.'

She wouldn't worry about it. It was her badminton night and the kids were over at her mother's. Paul decided that when he'd written that cheque out at the Country Club he'd get plastered in the bar. Heather would be using the car anyway and the walk home would do him good, provided he got there in a straight line.

34

The following Saturday Paul and Heather Channing attended the dinner dance at the Country Club.

'The usual crowd of bores,' thought Paul. 'Money orientated, class conscious buffoons!'

Heather had chosen to wear an extremely tight fitting dress and Paul thought she ought to have known better at her age. She sank more than her usual quota of martinis before dinner and by the time she had demolished the wine at table, didn't need much persuading to mount the dance floor with Clive Naylor-Drummond. CND, as he was known, was captain of the local rugby team. A lot younger than the Channings with a dubious reputation. The local vet leaned across the table to Paul.

'You want to watch young Drummond, old boy. Fancies his chances and gets a measure of success, they say.'

'Really,' said Paul. 'How very interesting!'

The vet gave a nervous laugh.

'Only joking Paul, I meant no offence to Heather.'

'Didn't you? Excuse me.'

With that he rose and made towards the boys room just as Heather was beginning to make an exhibition of herself on the dance floor. The other couples were clapping hands and giggling as she gyrated and postured, much to her partner's delight. When Paul returned to the table, Heather was in deep conversation with the vet and his wife. Paul was on the warpath.

'Better get you home dear before you get as drunk as a fiddler's bitch.'

Heather looked equally belligerent.

'Oh come off it, I'm just beginning to enjoy myself – for once.'

Vet and spouse looked uncomfortable. Paul didn't like scenes in public.

'All right Heather. I'm going to get a breath of fresh air. Slow down a bit, please.'

Heather raised her glass in defiance and Paul made for the exit. The night was clear and he stood near the entrance admiring the stars. He decided to stretch his legs and took a stroll towards the car park. When he got there, he did some more admiring – other people's expensive cars.

'Where the hell do they get the money from?' he thought.

When he drew level with his aged Vauxhall he swore. The front off-side tyre was flat – the near side one was hissing. There were marks on it. He knew his tyres had been slashed. Only his car had been singled out. None of the expensive models had been touched. He went straight back to the club entrance and made two telephone calls. The first to the police, the second to a taxi firm. When he eventually returned to the dinner table, Heather was dancing again, this time with the club secretary. When she returned to the table Paul told Heather what had happened.

'Charming! What it is to have friends,' she sneered.

Paul came close to slapping his wife and it must have shown. The club secretary swallowed hard.

'Oh Paul. I'm sorry. Is there anything I can do?'

'No thanks, Major. I'll have to wait until the police get here. I've ordered a taxi for midnight.'

The secretary put a hand on Paul's arm.

'In that case you won't be driving home. Let me get you both a drink.'

Paul declined and said his wife had sunk enough to float a battleship. Heather jutted her chin out.

'Bollocks,' she said very loudly.

This raised a few titters from the couples at the next table. The secretary winced. Heather was saved by the appearance at the dining entrance of a uniformed police constable.

'Streuth, they get younger every year,' thought Paul.

Although youngish, the constable was business-like. As he and Paul knelt to look at the tyres in the car park, torchlight revealed what had happened.

'A small hacksaw by the looks of it,' said the constable. 'There are vandals in the manor, Mr Channing. My bet is they were disturbed during the act. You could have lost all four. I'd better check for windscreen wipers and wing mirrors elsewhere.'

This he did and Paul accompanied him. No damage was evident to any other vehicle. Paul made towards the club entrance.

'I've got a taxi ordered for midnight, officer. Thank you for being so prompt.'

The young constable looked sympathetic.

'That's all right, sir. This will be reported in the morning.

To have your car vandalised alone like this is a little odd.'

Paul had already given his business address to the constable and now added his residential one with phone number. As the patrol car drew out of the club drive, Paul took a deep breath and re-entered the club to retrieve Heather. When he arrived, the vet was alone at the table.

'Oh Paul, Heather was upset, all this business about the tyre slashing, police etc. The major took her home. We didn't know how long you would be.'

Paul gave the vet a dirty look.

'She could have bloody well waited. All right, I'll cancel that taxi and walk home.'

There were many thoughts in Paul's mind as he walked home. His marriage was breaking up for a start, with all the implications that involved. This incident tonight was a measure of hate. After all these years! We, the British, so smug in our sense of superiority only imagined it was the foreign enemy who was capable of atrocity. Was there a raging beast in all men, waiting, just waiting to be let loose? Given the same sense of fear, violence and revenge, the kicking to death of an enemy at Plover's Green became a reality to Paul Channing. It also became an obsession.

When Paul opened the front door of his home he went straight to the lounge. Not bothering to mount the stairs, he lay gently on the settee. He was asleep within minutes. He wasn't to know it, of course, but the Russian bluff had been called. The Soviets turned back from Cuba that night. The world was safe, for a little longer.

5

During the weeks that followed Paul Channing's problems in Tallingwood, I began to have a few of my own in Rheindahlen. I was nominated to conduct a summary of evidence at Gutersloh, acting as junior member of the board. The president was a peppery wing commander, notorious for his bad manners. He seemed to find fault with everyone who worked for him, particularly me. Every statement we took had to be re- written time and time again. After a week at Gutersloh, in the clutches of this old ogre, I was glad to get back to Rheindahlen for a weekend's break. I met Dieter in the corridor outside SASO's office just before 5 pm and he grinned.

'What's up with you, Michael? Look as black as a cumulo-nimbus!'

I told him about my week locked in mortal combat with the old wing-co.

'Old dog and young dog by the sound of it,' said Dieter. 'By the way, I've had a reply from the Bundes Post about Neumann senior. Assuming you are in a fit state to take an interest in such things, do you want to hear what they said?'

I said I could do with a spot of light relief and took Dieter back to my office. My two colleagues there were preparing to leave and they gave me the keys to lock up. One of them asked how things were in Gutersloh. I said it was nearly as bad as the Cuban missile crisis.

'Oh yeah,' said my questioner. 'That old sod Aitken I suppose, thinks he's still instructing at the staff college! Cheers, have a good weekend, I reckon you've earned it!'

I put the kettle on and Dieter rang Lotte to let her know he would be home in half an hour.

'Right then', he said, putting down the receiver. 'Alfred Neumann retired from the Bundes Post in 1945 due to ill health. His pension continued to be paid until his death in

1946. According to records his address was listed as 8 Kaiser-weg, Salmisch, Nieder Bayern. Remembering the Rot-Kreuz information, this Salmisch address was probably the family home so I wrote a brief letter. A reply arrived in this morning's post. The people there now said the place had changed hands several times in recent years. They were München-leute, Munich people, and didn't know the Neumanns at all. They suggested we contact a Polizei-Meister Uhlbracht of the Bavarian Land Polizei at Salmisch and included his telephone number. So I rang him. Uhlbracht was out but his wife was helpful. She told me her husband would have known the Neumanns, being Salmisch born and bred, and suggested that I rang again after lunch. This I did and Uhlbracht wanted to know quite a lot about me and my reasons for ringing before he told me a damn thing.'

Dieter paused to sip his coffee. 'I told him about you, the pastor of your church and the war grave there. He listened to all this and said we would have trouble finding any relatives now. When Neumann senior died in 1946, he was being looked after by his youngest daughter. She sold up the house and moved out of Salmisch and hasn't been heard of since, as far as Uhlbracht knew. He would ask around the village among some of the older families just in case, though. That's the best we can hope for Michael.'

I said that if Uhlbracht had been a Salmischer all his life, he could have told us a lot more than he did.

Dieter smiled.

'Yes Michael, perhaps he could have done but these country boys are a cagey lot. Maybe he wanted somebody else's permission before telling us more.'

'Or maybe he just feels like Lotte,' I added, 'that the war is best forgotten.'

Dieter nodded.

'Uh-huh, there's always that of course. Uhlbracht sounded old enough to have been in the war and my experience has been that most veterans don't mind discussing that topic. Just one thing I've been meaning to ask you, why did you ask Bennecker if he saw any parachutes leaving Neumann's Zer-stoerer?'

I wanted to be careful answering this one.

'Well it was Baumbach, Neumann's gunner. It's odd that he

isn't buried in the same place. I'm going to write to the War Graves Commission again and ask if they have a record of Baumbach for 9 September 1940. If they were able to identify Neumann, presumably from his discs, then they should have been able to do the same with Baumbach.'

Dieter thought for a moment.

'I'm not sure what kind of dog-tags the crews wore in those days. I expect they were the usual kind. A waterproof green and a fireproof red. Even then, it's quite possible they could have been overlooked, you know.'

I had to agree with Dieter.

'Yes, in the rush to clear up the mess. I wonder just how diligent the police, firemen and CD crews were. Not that there could have been much left of anything. At a terminal velocity of about 300 mph – engines running nearly red hot and enough fuel to get back to Crécy!'

Dieter looked at his watch.

'I'd better be getting home now, Michael. Die Königen will be getting restive.'

I thanked him for all his help and said I'd like to invite them both out to dinner one evening, as soon as I found a partner to make up a foursome.

Dieter started to tease me.

'Got your eagle eye on that new red-headed WRAF officer just posted in?'

I said it was a good idea and I'd let him know if I had any luck in that direction.

When Dieter left I tidied up a few loose ends. Put the summary of evidence papers away and checked the combination lock of the safe.

When I got back to the mess I sat down to write that letter to the War Graves Commission. I put it in the post box on my way in to dinner and forgot all about it.

A week later Dieter rang and said that as Lotte was off to Cologne Cathedral that day with the Wives' Club, he was lunching in the mess. Much to his surprise, a letter had arrived from Uhlbracht in Salmisch yesterday.

'He must have got the go-ahead from somebody down there, Michael. What he says makes interesting reading.'

I was pleased to hear this and agreed to meet Dieter in the bar at 1 pm.

As we stood sipping our lagers in a quiet corner, the gist of Uhlbracht's letter was revealed by Dieter.

'The daughter who disappeared was last heard of in München. Her name was Inge. She married a man much older than herself who owned, among other things, a private secretarial agency, Franz Weber by name. There was another sister, Trudi. She was older than both Inge and her brother Kurt and always deeply religious. She entered a convent in Passau as a novitiate in 1941, and became a full member of the Carmelite Order there a few years later. So, we have a nun on our list now! What we must do is check the Munich business phone directory and see if we can trace these Webers. After that, we can ask Father Heussinger, the RC priest who comes here regularly, to see if he can help us with the Carmelites of Passau!'

I thought we were lucky to get this information.

'We seem to be getting warm, Dieter. You've done so well! I've a strong feeling we're going to solve this. By the way, if you and Lotte are free next Saturday, Margaret McKinnon the Titian-haired beauty from Intelligence has agreed to join us for dinner!'

Dieter's grin was enormous.

'You sly dog, a conquest no less, I'll be bound.'

'Not at all,' I said. 'She's a Scots lassie from Aberdeen and no nonsense.'

'With that figure?' chuckled Dieter.

I wasn't going to let him get away with that.

'Shame on you, Ewalt, you had better behave yourself or Lotte will part your hair with a rolling pin!'

Dieter laughed and said he'd get some sitters organised for the kids. He'd tell Lotte about it when she got back from Cologne. With that we went to lunch.

The following day I received a reply to my letter from the War Graves Commission. They said there was no record of a Baumbach interment for the date in question. They pointed out, however, that over a hundred graves bore the inscription 'Unknown German Airman' and there were five such cases listed on 9 September 1940. The graves were located at Maidstone, Brookwood, Brendan Hill, Coulsdon and Walton-on- Thames. They were sorry there was nothing more. I thought that they had done extremely well. It was the Coulsdon grave that caught my eye. That was the nearest to Tallingwood. It was high time I dropped a line to Paul Channing. I would suggest that Paul rang the commission and ask which church it was in Coulsdon where the Unknown was laid to rest. He could have a word with the vicar and take it from there. I began to think over Bennecker's account of the air battle. Spiral dive and 'G' forces not withstanding, my bet was that Baumbach managed to get out of that Messerschmitt. From his position, he would have seen the pilot was beyond help and summoning up enough superhuman strength in a state of terror, baled out while there was still enough time and height to do so. His parachute would have drifted in descent. The question was, where did he make his landfall? Was he so wounded himself that he died? Wasn't he wearing his ID tags? That landfall question again. Where was it? Coulsdon? Or, good grief, was it Plover's Green? Over to you Paul Channing, over to you indeed.

I booked a table at Karminski's in Düsseldorf for the Saturday and Dieter and Lotte picked Margaret and I up from the mess. We had an excellent dinner and I noticed with some amusement that Lotte looked even more stunning than usual. Quite a few male heads turned in admiration as Die Königen sailed in. Margaret McKinnon wore a very discreet outfit, as befitting a true daughter of Scotland. She got on well with Lotte; most women did. It turned out that Margaret had read Russian for her degree at St Andrews University. Lotte had tried to learn the same language at night school but found the grammar complicated. Margaret started to tease me then.

'You know they run interpreters' courses in the service, Mike. All at vast public expense! You've got a choice of Arabic, Chinese or Russian. The Russian course at London University ends up with six months in Paris – residence with White Russian families, just up your street, I'd say Mike!'

'It would certainly be up mine,' said Dieter.

Lotte smiled sweetly.

'And mine too, Liebchen.'

Margaret said, in view of the costs involved, married officers went to Paris unaccompanied.

'That lets you out then, doesn't it,' I said to Dieter.

The girls exchanged knowing glances and Lotte winked at Margaret.

Karminski's had a very good pianist and a few couples started to make use of the dance space. Lotte fixed me with one of her regal looks.

'Well, Michael Kendrick – aren't you going to ask me to dance?'

This omission was rectified and Dieter led Margaret out after us. When Lotte and I started our night-club shuffle, there wasn't much room to do anything else, she started.

'I like Fräulein Margaretta, she's very attractive and intelligent. A rare combination! I think she likes you Michael. Another woman can tell.'

I must have looked startled at this.

'Lotte, are you match-making again? If so, half the unattached officers in the mess are trying to date Margaret. I was just lucky, that's all.'

Lotte looked amused.

'I'm glad you think so, Michael. It's high time you settled down. Don't let this opportunity slip through your fingers! By the way, Dieter seems to be spending a lot of his time these days digging up the past. I hope matters will be resolved soon, so we can all get back to the present.'

I told Lotte then that we were close to winding things up. As I expected, she knew all about the Uhlbracht letter from Bavaria.

'Call it what you will, Michael, a woman's intuition perhaps but, have you really told us everything about the Neumann case? Was there something a little unusual about it?'

I felt most uneasy when she said this.

'I don't know all the facts, Lotte. Twenty-two years is a long time. It is interesting, though, and all I can say is that I'm lucky again, that Dieter finds it equally interesting. I'm more than grateful to him and you too, for letting it happen, Lotte dear!'

'All right Michael, we'll say no more – for the moment,' she replied. 'That husband of mine is making your Margaret laugh a little too much! Come on! We'll break those two up!'

We exchanged partners and rounded off the evening well. When Dieter and Lotte dropped us off at the mess, Margaret McKinnon turned to me in the foyer.

'I had a super evening, Mike. It's so good for us to get back to normal with Germany. I liked the Ewalts a lot. Thank you –

so much.'

I said it was my pleasure, thanked her for coming and hoped we could make up a foursome again. I was somewhat taken by surprise when Margaret leaned forward and gave me a demure peck on the cheek, and then she was gone.

'Hardly a conquest by Dieter's reckoning,' I thought. 'Nice girl, very nice. I must write to Paul Channing tomorrow, without fail.'

I still had other things on my mind.

6

Paul Channing sat reading my letter in his office while Millie Watkins clattered away on her typewriter next door. He was still wondering about that interview a week ago with an Inspector Truscott of Croydon CID. Truscott had arrived at the *Times* office unannounced. He said the statement taken from Paul, as given to Detective Constable Barber of Tallingwood, referred to some threatening letters. Barber had taken them and Truscott had now read them.

'We have to consider the possibility, Mr Channing, that whoever slashed your tyres could have written some of those letters. Most of them are pretty basic and well laced with obscenities. Are you quite sure you've no idea who wrote them?'

Paul narrowed his eyes.

'If I had, Inspector, I would have told the DC when he called. We get a fair measure of poison pen letters in the newspaper business. My reporter even gets abuse. Occupational hazard.'

'Perhaps the press asks for it at times, Mr Channing?'

Paul was beginning to bridle.

'This isn't one of the national daily papers, we don't go in for sensational journalism here. It's all mundane stuff. Nothing we have printed could possibly give offence to anyone. Despite that we still get our annual quota of nutters writing in.'

'All right' said Truscott. 'Then let's consider it's all directed at you on a personal level. Made any enemies recently – say socially?'

Paul said he hadn't.

'Barber tells me you've been doing some research into the war years here. One of your letters refers to you as a Kraut lover, Mr Channing. May I ask why?'

Paul told the inspector about the war grave and the vicar's

wish to trace the relatives.

'Well, you won't find them in Tallingwood, will you. Why so many questions around the manor?'

Paul replied that he felt it necessary to find out as much as he could about the circumstances of the case. If relatives were found they were bound to ask questions.

Truscott nodded.

'And what have you found, Mr Channing?'

'Not a great deal,' said Paul. 'There seems to be a general reluctance to discuss it. These letters and the tyre slashing seem to indicate that in some quarters, at least, I've upset a few people.'

'Yes,' said Truscott. 'I'm glad you see that. You won't be printing anything about this, I trust?'

Paul felt the real reason for Truscott's visit was beginning to emerge.

'Who sent you here, Inspector? Your colleagues of Special Branch?'

Truscott smiled.

'What a vivid imagination you have, Mr Channing. Why on earth should the Special Branch have an interest in all this?'

Paul was losing his temper.

'For the simple reason there may have been a cover-up re the circumstances of that German's death. A legal, medical and political cover-up that's been going on for years. I suspect that there are some people who would not regard the revelation of the facts to be in the public interest.'

Truscott kept smiling.

'So, it's the legend of Plover's Green that's bugging you. Barber told me about that too. Believe me Mr Channing, that's all that was, just a silly rumour put about by a few who wished it really did happen. As far as the public interest is concerned, I don't think any of this would reflect too well on the good people of Tallingwood. If this nasty little tale ever got to the press – just think of the damage it could do. If you don't print it, I can think of a few in Fleet Street who might be tempted to. My purpose in coming here was twofold. Firstly, I wanted to sound out your intentions re publication and secondly, to offer you some advice. I don't want you running the risk of personal injury from some nut case who doesn't like Germans. I'm too busy as it is without conducting enquiries of that sort.'

Paul wasn't convinced.

'If it'll make you feel any better, I've no intention of printing anything about this. It may surprise you but there are journalists with a sense of responsibility. These are my people here in Tallingwood and I'm not likely to print anything that reflects badly upon them. As for a possible punch up with the anti-German faction, I'm quite capable of looking after myself, thank you.'

Truscott rose slowly from his chair.

'I hope you are, Mr Channing. Stay away from pubs, dark alleyways and walking out alone. If you get any more unpleasant letters, make sure DC Barber sees them won't you?'

Paul's phone rang and Truscott said he would see himself out. The call was an advertising query and when it was dealt with Paul sat back to reflect on the inspector's visit. To be fair to Truscott, Paul knew that Croydon was Divisional HQ for the area. This would explain some things, but by no means all. The more he thought about it, the more convinced he became that the Plover's Green story was a fact. He was further convinced that Truscott had called to find out how much Paul really knew and then, to try and scare him off.

'At whose behest, I wonder?' thought Paul.

That was a week ago and now he sat studying the contents of my letter.

When he had finished reading it he put a call through to the War Graves Commission in London. The number was engaged, so he buzzed Millie Watkins on the office intercom.

'Miss Watkins, will you try this number for me a bit later? It's engaged at the moment and I want to finish the editorial comment for Friday's edition.'

He gave Millie the number – she took it with a sigh.

'These London numbers are dreadful in the mornings, Mr Channing. You may not get it till after lunch!'

Paul said he was prepared for that and asked Millie when she wanted to take her lunch break.

'As soon as I've completed this mass of accounts and bills' was her retort.

'All right' said Paul, leave it until this afternoon then. Must get our priorities right.'

There was a faintly discernable sniff on the other end of the intercom. Then it clicked off.

Paul lit a cigarette.

'So help me,' he thought, 'I'll swing for that old bat one day. If she wasn't so bloody efficient – I'd sack her.'

Just after 3pm the call to the War Graves Commission was made. Paul got through to the section dealing with the German side and explained he was ringing on my behalf, referring to the letters recently exchanged. He asked for the name of the church or cemetery in Coulsdon where the unknown war grave was located. After a long pause he was told it was plot 518 in the large cemetery attached to the borough crematorium. The woman at the end of the line added that the cemetery was a very large one and locating the grave would take time. She suggested Paul called in to the chapel of rest near the main entrance. The supervisor there had a chart of the cemetery and this would save some shoe leather.

Paul was obliged. He put down the receiver, got up and took his rain coat off the hook. As he passed through the outer office he turned to Millie Watkins.

'I'll be out for about an hour. I'm sure you'll hold the fort as well, if not better than I would. If anything important crops up, I'll attend to it when I get back.'

Millie frowned.

'If it's anything urgent, Mr Channing, can I get hold of you?'

'Yes, I'll be at the supervisor's office, Coulsdon Borough Cemetery.'

He gave Millie the phone number, checked his car keys and strode out. It was a nice afternoon. He wanted to get out of the office anyway. A group of children were on their way home from school and some of them were singing.

'Wish I was your age again,' thought Paul. 'Not a care in the world, any of you.'

The run to Coulsdon was pleasant. Paul drove up to the chapel of rest and parked his Vauxhall, now resplendent with two new front tyres in the forecourt. He entered the hall and tapped respectfully on the door marked 'Supervisor'. A grey-haired man in thick horn rimmed spectacles opened the door. Paul introduced himself, explained the reason for his call and asked if the supervisor could spare him a few minutes.

'Yes I think so, we've had the last cremation for the day.

Come in. What a beautiful day it is. Too good to be stuck in an office.'

The supervisor was middle aged, friendly and seemed to be the cooperative type. Paul sat down and explained further.

'The German war grave here being listed as "Unknown" poses certain problems. You wouldn't have had any visitors from Germany, of course. I was wondering what the borough records have to say about the matter. I'm currently dealing with a "known grave" in Tallingwood. It bears the same date as yours and we are in the process of tracing relatives in Bavaria at present.'

The supervisor looked mildly surprised.

'Well, that's a nice Christian gesture. I hope the relatives appreciate it. Ever been to Runnymede, Mr Channing?'

Paul admitted he hadn't and the supervisor continued.

'It's a beautiful memorial. The names of 22,000 Allied airman are recorded there. None of them have any known graves at all. I wonder how much research was ever done finding out what happened to them!'

Paul ignored the mild reproof.

'The Germans look after the RAF cemeteries extremely well – in the Federal Republic at least. A lot of Luftwaffe graves in this country are in a state of disrepair. The main reason being, the village churches just don't have the money for adequate upkeep.'

'Yes,' replied the supervisor, 'that would explain the removal of ours to Staffordshire next year. A good idea, I suppose, to put them all in one place. They should be properly tended in that case. I don't have very much on our grave at all.'

He opened a filing cabinet and drew out a card.

'It just says the remains of a German airman found at Acre Lane, Coulsdon on 9 September 1940, duly interred at the cemetery by the Imperial, now Commonwealth, War Graves Commission on 11 September. That's all it says. Nothing about an aeroplane crashing, like your case in Tallingwood.'

Paul thought for a moment.

'I don't suppose you know anybody who might have been around in those days? Preferably from Acre Lane?'

The supervisor blinked.

'Well, I certainly wasn't. Too busy chasing Italians in Libya. Wait a minute, yes, there is somebody in Acre Lane I know. Dreadful old bore, used to be an air raid warden, never stops talking about the Blitz.'

Paul pricked up his ears at this.

'Got a name and address?'

The supervisor scratched his head.

'Er, yes, Overton, Arthur Overton. Last house on the right at the end of the lane. Don't know the number, I'm afraid.'

Paul said he was grateful to the supervisor for all his help and asked if Overton was still working.

'Oh no, been retired for some years. If you want a chat about the war, he'll have a captive audience. You won't get away from him for hours, I warn you!'

Paul chuckled and shook hands on taking his leave. As they walked towards Paul's car, the supervisor glanced quickly at his visitor.

'Don't forget what I said about Runnymede, Mr Channing. My younger brother's name is recorded there. He was a sergeant observer in a Wellington. We lost him in 1942. His name was Peter Willis, he was just twenty.'

Paul didn't know what to say really.

'I'll remember that Mr Willis, I'll see what can be done. Thanks for all your help.'

Paul got into his car and drove off towards Acre Lane. When he arrived, he parked his car outside the last semi-detached house on the right-hand side. He rang the bell, which resulted in a furious outburst of dog barking. A chain rattled on the other side of the door and an elderly man peered around it. An aggressive Jack Russell dog poked its muzzle round the door, lower down. Paul introduced himself, said he'd just been to the cemetery and spoken to a Mr Willis, who thought that Mr Overton might be able to help with some research into the war, namely the Blitz.

'Ang on a mo, mate' said Overton. 'Jason 'ere don't like strangers, I'll 'ave to put 'im in the back yard. I'll be back in a mo.'

The front door was promptly shut and Paul waited patiently until it was re-opened. Overton ushered Paul into the lounge.

'Watcha want ter know then? Been over a long time nah the war. Seems to bore everybody.'

Paul explained his interest in the Coulsdon war grave.

'Blimey, the war really is over, innit? Bad business that at poor old Ethel's place. She went 'dahn the garden to bring in her Monday wash and found it lying there.'

Paul wanted to get his facts straight.

'Ethel you say?'

'Yes,' said Overton. 'Ethel Brown as lived at number twenty-two. Widder woman she was. 'Ad a son in the Pioneer Corps. Lived on 'er own in them days.'

Paul took this in and continued.

'What exactly was it she found in her garden, Mr Overton?'

Overton swallowed hard.

'A flying 'elmet. Poor Ethel was in bleedin 'isterics when I got there. She 'ad to be sedated you know by the doctor.'

Fearing the worst Paul asked why.

Overton took a deep breath.

'There was a bloke's 'ead still in it, that's why mate! The RAF identified it from Kenley. I seed it miself. It was a buff coloured one with brown leather ear pieces, they said only Jerries wore them. Gawd knows what 'appened to the rest of 'im, poor bleeder.'

Paul knew why the Coulsdon grave was listed as unknown. He didn't want to hear anymore.

'I'm sorry Mr Overton, I'm not feeling very well, please excuse me.'

Overton protested.

'Don't you want to know anyfink else? Stop for a cuppa at least.'

Paul said he would come back again later in the week when he felt better.

Overton looked aggrieved.

'I may not be at 'ome.'

Paul said he would take a chance on that and thanked Overton for his help. He was seen to the door by his host, who felt cheated out of a long chin-wag about the Blitz.

On the drive back to Tallingwood, Paul wondered about Baumbach, Neumann's gunner. He'd only pretended to be sickened by Overton's story. He just wanted to get away from the old boy.

'Bloody hell' he thought. 'What a shambles that battle on the 9th must have been. That helmet in Mrs Brown's garden might have been Baumbach's, I suppose. With all those planes buzzing around, as Mike says in his letter, that gunner might

51

have been chopped up by a propeller. On the other hand, so many other enemy planes were knocked down that day. A lot of them were bombers. If they were caught carrying their loads, I suppose Mike would know about that.'

When Paul finally drew up outside the *Times* office it was gone 5 pm. Millie Watkins didn't like working late.

'Just one call from the Chamber of Commerce, Mr Channing. They didn't care for your coverage of their last conference. Will you ring a Mr Marshall in the morning please? He wants some amendments in our next week's edition.'

Paul said he would, adding that he would finish up at the office if Millie wanted to get away as there was no need to hang on.

When he sat down at his desk again, he saw another letter lying there – unstamped, addressed to the Editor, *Tallingwood Times*. When he opened it, the contents were brief.

'If you want to know what happened at Plover's Green in 1940 – meet me in the Public Bar of the White Hart this Saturday at 9 pm. Don't ring your friends of the Fuzz, or you'll find out bugger all.' Signed 'A Friend.'

Ringing his so called 'friends of the Fuzz' is exactly what Paul ought to have done, but he didn't. He wanted to handle this on his own. That was mistake number one. Intending to call in at the White Hart on Saturday was mistake number two. Somebody in Tallingwood knew what had happened at Plover's and Paul was determined to find out about it, risks or no risks. If only I had been on leave then, I would have made damn sure Messrs Barber and Truscott were around when we went. I wasn't to learn what happened to Paul for several weeks. Too busy with my own petty problems at Rheindahlen then, and I've blamed myself for that – ever since.

7

Dieter Ewalt managed to acquire a Munich business directory and discovered two entries under the name Weber Gmb. He dismissed the first of these as it was an electrical engineering company. The second, however, was listed as a publishing house so he put a call through and spoke to one of the secretaries. He asked the young woman if there were any links between the publishing house and a private secretarial agency under the same name. She said there wasn't but remembered such an agency a few years ago, having registered with it herself at the time. She went on to say that it was run by a Frau Weber then, but had heard the firm was sold later. The buyers were Neckermanns and if Dieter would hold the line she would give him the number to ring. Dieter jotted it down and when he got it, thanked the girl and dialled the new number. A man answered and Dieter said he was trying to get in touch with a Frau Weber who, he believed, had sold the agency to Neckermanns. The man wanted to know Dieter's reason for seeking Frau Weber, so he told a white lie, saying he was conducting enquiries on behalf of the Soldaten Friedhof Organisation, adding that Frau Weber's brother was lost during the war. The man asked Dieter to hang on and after a lengthy wait a woman answered. She said that Inge Weber had sold the agency on the death of her husband and having established a good reputation in her own field, was offered an extremely good job in Düsseldorf. She believed the firm that Frau Weber went to was Kleinerts. That was some time ago. Dieter thanked the woman and immediately went for the local directory.

'Well, well,' he thought to himself, 'if Inge Weber is still in Düsseldorf, how very convenient.'

He soon found Kleinerts in the directory and put a call through. The girl on the switchboard put Dieter on to an extension where he asked for Frau Weber. Yet another woman answered and Dieter had to repeat his white lie.

'I'm Frau Weber's secretary. She's away on business at the moment,' said the woman. 'If you care to leave your number Herr Ewalt, I will see she gets the message.'

Dieter left his number at Rheindahlen and hoped Inge Weber lived in Düsseldorf, this very much to himself. When his call was finished, he thumbed through the Düsseldorf directory. Finally he found what he was looking for. From the address, it looked as if Inge Weber was living in a classy area of the city. A flat by all accounts. He would try her at Kleinerts tomorrow and failing that, ring her at home one evening. Dieter suddenly remembered that Father Heussinger, the Roman Catholic priest from Munchen Gladbach, came to Rheindahlen on Friday evenings to attend to the spiritual needs of the RCs on the base. Father Heussinger took confession and Dieter rather liked him, despite the fact he wasn't a Catholic. They had met in the mess some months ago. Realising today was a Friday, Dieter would go to the RC church that evening and see if he could have a word with the good priest. Lotte would want to know about it of course. When he got home at the end of the working day, he told her. Much to Dieter's surprise, Lotte was calm.

'All right Dieter, neither of us will get any peace until you have found those relatives. Go ahead and play *Emil and the Detectives* for all I care. As if this war business wasn't bad enough, here you are, off to consult with the Church of Rome! Just remember, we are Lutherans, Liebchen!'

Dieter said he wouldn't forget, leaned over the table and kissed his wife. Then he went into the lounge to chat to his children.

Knowing that confession began at 6 pm Dieter thought it prudent to get down to the RC church at 7 pm. This he did and, on arrival, only one penitent sat waiting in the pew. The confession took ten minutes and finally Father Heussinger came out of the box. He caught sight of Dieter and exclaimed.

'I don't believe it! Don't tell me you've decided to become a convert?'

Dieter gave him one of his broad grins.

'No Father, nothing so dramatic! Can you spare me a few minutes please?'

The priest sat down on the pew beside Dieter.

'Of course, my son. What is it?'

They were completely alone in that little prefabricated church-cum-chapel and Dieter told Father Heussinger everything about the Neumann case, Uhlbracht's letter from Bavaria and the possible need to get in touch with the Carmelite nuns of Passau. Father Heussinger listened intently throughout. When Dieter had finished, instead of making any immediate reply he suddenly knelt, made the sign of the cross and Dieter didn't know quite what to do. It was obvious that the priest was in prayer. He didn't take long over it. Settling back in the pew, the priest turned to Dieter.

'The Carmelites are a very strict order, my son. I will do what I can to help you. Your British friend – this Michael Kendrick, would he go all the way down to Passau if a meeting could be arranged, you think?'

Dieter nodded.

'I know he would, Father, and I would go with him.'

The priest took a small note book from his soutane.

'Leave me your phone number, Dieter, I'll ring you.'

This was done and the two men took their leave. Father Heussinger locked the chapel doors and shook hands with Dieter.

'How's Lotte, by the way?'

'She's fine, Father, just fine, thank you.'

The priest smiled and was gone. Dieter walked back to his married quarter, feeling he had, at least, done something useful that day.

On his way home Dieter thought about Kleinerts in Düsseldorf. He knew they were one of the biggest travel agencies in West Germany. With the strengthening Deutschmark and car ownership on the increase, the German people were beginning to become Europe's major tourists. If Inge Weber had such a good job with Kleinerts, she must have been good at languages. With so many West German business houses having close financial ties with London and New York, it was Dieter's bet she spoke good English.

'That would save a lot of time,' he thought.

When he arrived home, Lotte was upstairs with the children. She used to make them read a few pages before settling down for the night. When she came into the lounge, Dieter told her everything about his calls to Munich and Düsseldorf and his chat with Father Heussinger.

'Well, I hope Michael Kendrick is right,' said Lotte. 'The sooner we get this thing over with the better. He said you were near the end of it. By the way, there was a news flash on TV while you were out. Another F104 crash, somewhere off the coast of Heligoland.'

Dieter swore softly.

'That'll be Oldenburg again. Another trip up there, I expect. Oberst Letzlinger will want to go this time. He will probably ring this evening.'

Letzlinger did just that. It was arranged that Dieter and his Oberst would fly up to Oldenburg first thing on Monday morning. Dieter rang me in the mess that evening and told me about Inge Weber. As he was going to be away for a few days he wanted to know if I would care to call her at Kleinerts myself. Replying that I would feel a lot happier if we met Frau Weber together, Dieter said that would be all right provided I could wait a few days, maybe a week or more. I thought about this and then asked him for Kleinerts' number in Düsseldorf. This was given and Dieter said he would be surprised if Frau Weber did not speak fluent English; he explained about the travel agency side of things. I thanked him for his call and told him to behave himself while he was away.

He chuckled.

'I've got my "groupie" in tow on this trip Michael, not much chance to do anything else. Wiedersehen – old sausage.'

'Wiedersehen, old cock,' said I. 'Good luck up at Oldenburg, I do watch your TV, you know!'

Lotte then came on the line.

'Michael, do you think Margaret would be interested in a boat trip down the Rhine next week? Lots of wine, soft music, very romantic!'

I said I'd ask her and assumed this would be next Saturday. This was confirmed.

'I have to queue up, you know, Lotte' I added. 'Margaret's a highly sought-after young lady.'

It was Lotte's turn to chuckle.

'I don't think you will have any trouble, Michael. Just let me know before Wednesday please. I have to book the tickets.'

I agreed to do this and Dieter came back on the line.

'If you do ring Inge Weber at Kleinerts, Michael, I'm

supposed to be with the Soldaten Friedhof people, OK?'

No doubt Dieter had his reasons for this and I didn't query it. I thanked him again and put down the receiver. I went into the mess ante-room after that call and did some thinking. On due reflection I felt it would be best for Dieter to make the initial contact with Inge Weber. I was, after all, a serving officer in the Royal Air Force. Bearing in mind what happened to her brother and the great bomber offensives which followed later in the war, it seemed to me that the RAF could still evoke some hostile reactions from Germans. I would wait until Dieter's business in Heligoland was concluded. Far better for him to find out and if things were going to be sticky, I would give the matter some further thought.

On the following Monday morning, my own group captain called me into his office.

'What about your leave plans this summer, Kendrick?'

He had some papers on his desk which he started to look at. I always made a point of being brief with my replies to Groupie. He preferred it that way.

'Early September, sir.'

Groupie singled out one of his papers.

'We've got the Air Secretary's presentation team coming over in the first week of September. They are prepared for careers interviews after their talks. You are tour – ex next summer, you know. Ought to be thinking about your next posting. Don't let the grass grow under you feet.'

'No, sir.'

'Well,' said Groupie. 'At your age you won't be employed in the fighter ground-attack role any more. Chaps in their early thirties find themselves flying something a little more sedate. Could be the V-force, Maritime or even Transport. I would suggest you give it some thought.'

'Yes, sir.'

Groupie then took another paper from his selection.

'Wing Commander Aitken tells me your staff work needs a bit of brushing up. Those of us on ground tours are expected to be as efficient with org and admin as we are in the air.'

'Yes, sir,' said I, again thinking that I didn't join the service to be a bloody scrivener.

Groupie frowned.

'And don't look like that! The general duties aircrew branch means what it says, general duties, my lad. The taxpayers expect to get their money's worth, especially in peace time!'

'Yes, sir.'

Groupie leaned back in his chair.

'There may be an informal investigation for you to do at Laarbruch this week. I wouldn't want it to develop into a full blown court of inquiry. If it looks as if it may do, get some advice from Wing Commander Aitken.'

'Yes, sir,' thinking to myself 'Oh death, where is thy sting?'

Groupie wore the faintest trace of a smile.

'Try and show some enthusiasm, Kendrick. It's a simple enough case at Laarbruch. Service Land Rover damaged trying to avoid a civilian cyclist.'

'Yes sir, when would I be required to go?'

'I'll let you know soon enough. Meanwhile, I'd be obliged if you finished that NATO Op. order this morning! All right, that's it.'

'Yes, sir' said I, and inwardly fuming, went back to my own office. When I got there, one of my colleagues, George Bradley, looked up.

'Cheer up, mate! Groupie been giving you a hard time, has he?'

I sat heavily in my chair.

'No more than usual. That old sod Aitken's been tale-bearing on me over that summary of evidence we did.'

George grunted.

'Yes, you'd expect Groupie to take his side. Both war time wallahs, the pair of them. It's just the generation gap, Mike. They regard us as a bunch of spoiled schoolboys, which we were in the war, of course. I heard one old codger in the mess the other night sounding off about the likes of us: "No flak, no fighters, these youngsters don't know how lucky they are."'

I made a rude sign with one hand and reached for the Op Order papers with the other.

'With your permission, Flight Lieutenant, I'll get on with my chores. This thing's due to run the editorial gauntlet this afternoon.'

With that, we both got down to some work.

On Wednesday afternoon I was given my brief for Laarbruch and Groupie told me to get there first thing on Thursday morning.

'If you pull your finger out and get some coherent statements from everybody, you should be able to wind things up by
Friday afternoon. Don't forget what I told you about contact-
ing Wing Commander Aitken either. You know his extension
number, I suppose?'

I said I had it and very nearly added 'and I wish I hadn't.'
That more or less took care of the week. I was back in the mess
in time for dinner on Friday night and decided to pop into the
bar for a dry sherry to sharpen my appetite.

To my surprise Dieter and Oberst Letzlinger were caught in
deep conversation with two USAF officers. Dieter caught my
eye and winked. I hung on for a while in case this little group
broke up. It didn't, so I went into dinner. As I sat sipping my
coffee in the ante-room, Dieter appeared alone.

'Been chasing the birds at Laarbruch, I hear – there's no
end to your wickedness, is there?'

I said I was sorry for not ringing Lotte Wednesday about the
Rhine boat trip. With all the Laarbruch panic I'd forgotten
about it. Dieter said he would apologise on my behalf when he
got home. He had only just got back from Oldenburg.

'Look, we'll let the dust settle over the weekend, Michael.
I'll ring you early in the week. How's Margaret, by the way?'

I said I hadn't seen her and suggested she may have been
whisked away somewhere by one of those Intelligence branch
roués.

Dieter grinned.

'Never mind Michael. The path of true love seldom runs
smoothly. Give my regards when you do see her. Must rush off
now or Lotte will be on the warpath. See you.'

I sat back and finished my coffee, thinking that now Dieter
was back matters could proceed with the Neumann case. I
wondered what Inge Weber would be like, always assuming
she agreed to meet me. Time would tell.

☆   ☆   ☆

Major Max Litjens was Dieter Ewalt's immediate superior in
the division. He rang Dieter on the Monday and asked him to
call in.

Litjens offered Dieter a cigarette.

'You had a caller while you were away. Exchange put it

through to me in your absence. It was a woman from Kleinerts in Düsseldorf. She was ringing on behalf of her boss, a Frau Weber. She was under the impression we were the Soldaten Friedhof Offices.'

'Ah well.' said Dieter, 'I can explain all that.'

Litjens took a lungful of smoke.

'Good, I'm glad you can.'

Dieter gave a brief run down on the Neumann case and said, in view of the circumstances, he thought Frau Weber would be more likely to respond favourably to Soldaten Freidhof than she would to any joint Luftwaffe–RAF effort.

'I see,' said Litjens. 'Well, you might have let us know about it. Could have saved a lot of embarrassment. I think your caller was a bit taken aback when she realised she was on to Flight Safety Division here at Rheindahlen! Naturally enough I knew nothing about the reason for her call. I just took the number and said I'd get you to ring on your return.'

Dieter felt uncomfortable.

'My apologies, Herr Major. If it hadn't been a rush to get up to Heligoland with Oberst Letzlinger, I would have briefed Hauptmann Bauer.'

'Yes, all right' said Litjens, 'I trust you will make it clear to Kleinerts, Frau Weber or Mickey Mouse for that matter, that you are not working for Soldaten Friedhof!'

Dieter said he would make it quite clear. Litjens handed over the Kleinerts number and then asked Dieter about the Heligoland investigations. They sat discussing the case for twenty minutes and Dieter said the final draft report should be ready by Wednesday. Unlike similar cases recently covered, this one appeared to be pilot-error rather than technical failure. Litjens said he had heard as much already from Letzlinger. He thanked Dieter and wished to convey his compliments to Lotte. This was done with one of Litjens' rare smiles. With an inward sigh of relief Dieter went back to his own office. When he sat down at his desk he put a call through to the extension at Kleinerts that Litjens had given him. To his surprise it was answered by Inge Weber. Dieter took a deep breath.

'I must apologise, Frau Weber. This is Hauptmann Ewalt at Rheindahlen. There seems to have been some misunderstanding the other day. I have in fact been making enquiries on behalf of Soldaten Friedhof. I am not, of course employed by that organisation.'

There was a pause before Inge replied.

'Well then, Herr Ewalt, Bundes Luftwaffe, Soldaten Friedhof or whatever! May I ask you why you rang last week?'

'It's about your brother's grave in England, Frau Weber. The pastor of the church there asked a colleague of mine to make some enquiries in the hope of finding relatives.'

There was another pause from Inge.

'This colleague of yours, is he with Soldaten Friedhof?'

'Er, no, he isn't. He's been in touch with them of course through me. This friend of mine is British and he comes from the town where your brother is buried.'

'That's very kind of them,' said Inge. 'Such a long time ago, Herr Ewalt. We were unaware of our brother's resting place for some years. The Rot Kreuz people wrote to us after the war. For many reasons, we didn't answer their letter and I won't go into that now. I have thought about visiting the grave many times and perhaps one day I will. We never knew the exact circumstances of his death either. Would your British friend know anything about that, do you think?'

It was Dieter's turn to pause before answering.

'Yes, Frau Weber. He's done a certain amount of research on that. He also has some information on the re- interring of the grave to another part of England next year. I know he would like to meet you, if you think that's possible?'

'Does he speak German?'

Dieter coughed.

'Well, a little, yes. Understands more than he speaks. I expect your English is far better than his German.'

'Yes, it probably is. I get plenty of practice in this business. What is your friend's name and what does he do? You say he's a colleague.'

Dieter realised the moment of truth had arrived.

'Kendrick, Michael Kendrick. He's a British Air Force officer but, like me, of the post-war generation, Frau Weber.'

'So the RAF, then!' said Inge. 'Thank him for what he has done. I am extremely busy at the moment, Herr Ewalt. What did you have in mind re a meeting between us?'

'Both Kendrick and I would be pleased to invite you to dinner one evening in Düsseldorf, at any time it's convenient,' said Dieter.

'I'll see what I can do,' she replied. 'It won't be for a week or so. I have your number in Rheindahlen. Thank you for ringing.'

'Thank you, Frau Weber – I'll look forward to your call,' said Dieter and he heard the line click off at the other end.

'Hm,' thought Dieter to himself. 'She sounds a very brisk and business-like lady. Bit of cool cucumber, though! I'd better hold Michael's hand when we meet up with her, if we ever do!'

With that he carried on with the draft report on the Heligoland incident.

When he got home that night he told Lotte about his call to Düsseldorf and his personal impressions of Inge Weber.

'Well, good for her,' said Lotte. 'The women of this country are changing. No longer the downtrodden little things steeped in "Kirch, Kinder and Kuchen" anymore.'

Dieter smiled.

'Wonder what she looks like? Sounds like she might be something out of *Götterdämmarung*, all breast plates, horned helmet and brandishing a battle axe.'

Lotte giggled.

'Serve you right if she was! Do you think you'll ever hear from her again?'

'I just don't know at the moment,' said Dieter. 'She's got to digest everything first. She sounded a little strained at the mention of Michael's RAF background.'

'Yes,' said Lotte. 'Can't blame her for that. Any mention of her sister at all?'

'No, and I didn't raise that,' said Dieter. 'I'm still hoping that the good Father Heussinger will come up with something there. By the way, Max Litjens sends his compliments, we had a chat this morning.'

Lotte brightened up at this.

'Oh, that's nice. Poor Max, such a solemn soul.'

'Yes.' replied Dieter. 'You know he's called laughing boy Litjens in the mess?'

Lotte did know.

'He's just a serious type of man, Liebchen. Not like you at all. He's been through a bad time, remember? Losing his wife like that. He ought to marry again. Been on his own long enough.'

Dieter thought for a moment.

'I'll see if I can fix him up with the widow Weber, they'd make a good couple!'

Just as Lotte was about to respond to this outrageous suggestion the Ewalts' phone rang. Dieter answered it. It was Father Heussinger.

'Hello Dieter, hope you've had your evening meal?'

'Yes, thank you, Father.'

'I've had a brief letter from the mother superior in Passau. Sister Neumann is unwell, I'm afraid. Not been well for some time. The letter goes on to say that it would be unwise to remind Sister Neumann of the family tragedy during the war. There had been a dispute at home and there had been little or no contact between her and the younger sister. In any event, the order does not permit male visitors. It just ends by suggesting we continue with our search for the other sister, last heard of in München, under the married name of Weber.'

Dieter thanked his caller for the trouble he had taken and then told him of his call to Düsseldorf earlier in the day.

'Frau Weber gave a slight hint of something odd just after the war when the Rot Kreuz informed them about the grave's location. She said they didn't answer that letter and she didn't want to go into the reasons why.'

'Well,' said the priest. 'Perhaps when you meet her, she may tell you. If I can do anything to help Dieter, let me know, won't you?'

Dieter said he would.

When the call was over, Lotte wanted to know all about it.

'The plot thickens, then' she said. 'Nothing like a good old family row to last for years. I shouldn't think those two sisters had a lot in common. One to the church, the other to marriage and a successful business career. Don't expect Inge Weber to tell you much. Women don't confide in strangers as a rule. Not unless they're desperately lonely and unhappy. I don't think the younger sister falls into that category at all from your description.'

'No,' said Dieter. 'I'm sure you're right, Liebling. Thanks for your opinion, I value it. I haven't the faintest idea what to tell Michael Kendrick. Best to say nothing until we hear from Düsseldorf.'

Lotte agreed. She got up to put the coffee on and Dieter

turned to the TV to catch the evening news bulletin.

8

Tallingwood Grove is bordered by ash and elm trees. The lawns are well kept and on either side of the pathways the flower beds are always well stocked. At the far end of the Grove stands the war memorial. The dead of both wars are recorded on that stone work and looking down upon those names from above there stands a bronze figure. It is an infantryman, his rifle reversed with his head bowed in prayer. There are far more names recorded for the first war than for the second. Perhaps it is only fitting that the bronze figure is cast as a soldier of 1914–18. There were a few bench seats in the Grove and those that were there seemed to be placed in secluded spots beneath the trees. It was a favourite place in my young days and even now, well used by courting couples. It was just such a couple, in search of a quiet bench that night, who discovered Paul Channing. He was lying face down at the north end of the Grove not far from the exit. The boy thought at first that Paul had just flopped down there, probably the worse for drink. The girl didn't want to linger and protested when the boy went back to have a second look. As he turned Paul over, he felt the stickiness on his hands. He took out his Ronson lighter and lit it.

'Christ, Sue', the boy exclaimed. 'This bloke's badly hurt. We must get an ambulance and then call the fuzz.'

Sue didn't want anything to do with it and called the boy a silly bugger for sticking his nose in. The boy was made of sterner stuff.

'All right. You do what you like. I'm going to Tallingwood Green. There's a phone box there. We can't let him just lie here.'

Shamed into some sense of action, the girl went with the boy to Tallingwood Green and stood with him in the kiosk while he made the triple 9 calls. Having made them, Exchange told the boy to hold. The girl was crying and said she was going home.

'John, they'll say we did it! Your hands all over him. You must be crazy.'

The boy lost his patience.

'For Heaven's sake then, go home! You heard me give my name. There's no going back now, Sue.'

Exchange had put the boy through to Casualty at Tallingwood Cottage Hospital. The staff nurse on duty told the boy not to move the man he had found and that an ambulance was on its way. It would help if the caller stayed at the Grove entrance to assist the crew in finding the injured person. The boy agreed to do this.

'I've got to go back, Sue. You go home now. If the fuzz want to talk to you, just tell them the truth.'

The girl was in near hysterics.

'I'm not going home alone. I'm too scared! Fine bloody evening this turned out to be. We'll end up in cells at the local nick!'

The boy put his arm around the girl's shoulder.

'No we won't Sue. Come on. The fuzz never nicked anyone for telling the truth. That bloke needs attention and the sooner he gets it the better.'

☆ ☆ ☆

Inspector Truscott had just read a recent remand report when his phone rang. Mondays were always bad days and this was to be no exception. He lifted the receiver with a heavy sigh.

'Truscott.'

'Good morning, sir, it's DC Barber at Tallingwood.'

'Yes Barber. What is it?'

'We've had a bad case of assault here over the weekend. It's Channing – the bloke who had all those threatening letters. He's in the Cottage Hospital at the moment but they want to move him to Croydon General. He's still unconscious.'

Truscott grabbed his notebook.

'Any pre- lim on this? What about his wallet?'

'It's missing, sir, so it could have been a mugging.'

Truscott snorted.

'Yeah, and it could have been a lot of other things. Any leads?'

'Just a couple of kids who found him in the Grove.'

'Any idea where Channing had been?'

'It was Saturday night, late. I checked on all the local pubs and the landlord of the White Hart remembered him. Said he'd sat in the public bar for over an hour on his todd and then left around 10pm. Nobody had spoken to Channing and he drank nothing more than halves of bitter.'

'Waiting for someone, that's what he was doing,' said Truscott. 'OK Barber. Let me know as soon as he regains consciousness. I want to talk to Channing. If he comes to, get down there to the Cottage Hospital and conduct the usual enquiries. See how much Channing can remember of what happened at the Grove.'

'Yes sir. For what it's worth, I think they'll move him to Croydon General this afternoon. In that event, you'll be in a better position to interview him than I will.'

'Saucy young pillock,' thought Truscott.

'Thank you for your support, Constable,' said Truscott. 'I might be on your next promotion board – so watch it.'

Before Barber had a chance to profess his innocence, Truscott had replaced the receiver.

'That silly man,' he thought. 'I warned him. As the good Lord is my witness – I warned him. All this flitting about in Tallingwood. Stirring up the entire manor about the war and this bloody German in particular. Does it matter now – after all these years?'

At the back of Truscott's mind was another issue. He would keep it to himself for the time being. Firstly, he needed to talk to Paul Channing, whenever that might be. If he discovered the identity of the attacker or attackers, that could be the beginning of some real problems. He put a call through to an extension in London. It was engaged. He felt in need of a breath of fresh air. Folding up his papers, he made for the door and passing through the corridors, stopped at the main entrance. Turning to the duty sergeant, Truscott fumbled for his car keys.

'Tallingwood Cottage Hospital if anyone wants me, Sergeant.'

'Very good, sir,' said the sergeant. 'I'll take any in-coming calls for you. The chief superintendent said he wouldn't be back until about three.'

'That's a comforting thought,' said Truscott and the desk sergeant grinned. Two constables plus a youth, looking the worse for wear, suddenly appeared at the desk.

'What's this lot?' said the sergeant.

Truscott didn't want to hear the rest of it and kept on going. When he arrived at Tallingwood Hospital he showed his ID card to the nurse at Reception.

'I'd like to talk to the doctor in charge of the assault case. Name of Channing.'

The nurse took a good look at Truscott's card.

'If you wait, Inspector, I'll see if Doctor Freeman is available. He's very busy. I'd suggest you take a seat.'

Truscott didn't care for the medical profession in general and stroppy young nurses in particular.

'This is an urgent police matter,' said Truscott, looking ominous. 'Please tell Doctor Freeman that.'

The young nurse at reception didn't care much for dictatorial middle- aged males. They reminded her too much of her father

'I'll do what I can, Inspector. You will have to wait anyway.'

Truscott fixed one of his steely-eyed looks on the nurse.

'You saucy young mare,' he thought. 'Women! They're getting completely out of hand. What's got into them these days?' Then aloud, he added, 'All right, staff! I do have a job to do. A full report has to be written up on all this. You wouldn't like to come out of this in a poor light, I'm sure. I'll repeat what I've said, this is a matter of extreme urgency. Please act accordingly.'

The nurse chose to ignore Truscott's riposte. She pressed a button on her call box.

'Is Doctor Freeman likely to be available? I have an Inspector Truscott of Croydon CID at Reception. He wants to discuss the casualty admission on Saturday night. Name of, er, Channing.'

There was a lengthy pause, a voice on the other end said that Freeman was on his rounds at the moment but would be informed. Truscott heard this and turning his back on the nurse at Reception, went to sit down on one of the uncomfortable looking chairs, by courtesy of the NHS. He sat there for fifteen minutes and was about to leave in disgust when a tall figure wearing a white smock and a stethoscope suddenly appeared at reception. The nurst pointed to Truscott. The tall figure stepped forward.

'Good morning. Inspector Truscott? Sorry you've been kept waiting. Will you come into my office please. Place is in an uproar today, nothing unusual in that!'

Truscott felt relieved. The doctor was in his forties and looked the cooperative type. They went into a small office down the corridor and soon got down to business. The doctor was clearly rushed off his feet, did not waste words and came straight to the point.

'We were damn lucky with Channing. The ward sister on duty Saturday recognised him. She knows his wife well, you see. Without her help, goodness knows what we would have done. He had nothing on him to establish identity. He's regained consciousness, Inspector, but I'm afraid I'm still worried about him. Badly beaten up with broken ribs, contusions to the stomach, back and pelvis. The most important injury is to the head. Concussion is a most challenging area to us. We still don't know enough about it, I only wish we did. In my opinion, there is a risk of cerebral haemorrhage and if we are not very careful, Channing will suffer a relapse. For that reason I'm against moving him, although my superiors here don't agree. I could be wrong. Who am I to challenge thirty years of experience with my mere fifteen?'

Truscott took an immediate liking to Doctor Freeman. He had that rare quality for a man in his profession, humility.

'Thank you for that, Doctor,' said Truscott. 'What about Channing's wife? She knows all about this, I take it?'

'Oh yes,' said Freeman, 'she's been here since the early hours of Sunday morning. Stayed with her husband the whole time – that is, until we gave her something to sleep an hour ago. You won't be able to talk to either of them until tomorrow, Inspector, I'm sorry.'

Truscott took his notebook out.

'That's all right, Doctor, I quite understand. Thank you for being so helpful. How do you think Channing sustained his head injuries? Was it a deliberate blow to the head?'

Doctor Freeman thought.

'The ambulance crew said they found Channing lying close to a flower bed in Tallingwood Grove. They are all bordered by stones and according to the senior crew member, there were blood stains on them.'

'In other words, Doctor, Channing could have fallen heavily and sustained his injuries that way.'

'Yes, of course,' said Freeman and added with a smile, 'I'd say that – and I'm not in your business!'

Truscott stood up and said he would like to know if and when Channing was to be moved. Freeman replied that he would advise. With that, the doctor and the police inspector parted. Truscott walked down the passage and decided he didn't like the smell of hospitals. He didn't like the arrogance of the medical profession, particularly the distaff side. To be fair, Freeman was different. For just a moment he thought to himself.

'One in a hundred, that medic, I was lucky there at least!'

Truscott's next port of call was Tallingwood Police Station. He found DC Barber in the rest room taking a coffee break. Taking a cup himself, Truscott sat down beside Barber.

'Don't get up Barber, relax. I've just been to the hospital. Channing's come round now but we won't be able to question him for a while. Tell me about the statements you've taken so far.'

This Barber did, adding, 'The pub was pretty full that night. The landlord knew quite a number of the customers, the regulars, that is. I've taken statements from some of them but there are several outstanding. The landlord says Channing left the bar on his own and he did not remember anyone else leaving the same time or shortly after for that matter. The White Hart has an extension to 11 pm on Saturdays and the customers take full advantage of it.'

Truscott sipped his coffee.

'What about Mrs Channing – when did you contact her?'

'About 11.30 pm,' said Barber. 'Somebody at the hospital recognised Channing and Withers and Pollington went to inform her and took her in the patrol car. I arrived shortly after she did. She was badly shaken up by it all.'

'I see,' said Truscott. 'This ward sister who knows Mrs Channing, get anything out of her?'

'Not a lot,' replied Barber, 'except that she had heard the Channing's marriage was going through a rough patch. Nothing unusual in that.'

70

'No,' said Truscott. 'On the other hand, Channing might have had an extra marital going on. Arranged to meet his bit on the side and fell victim to a jealous husband, lying in wait for him. We might have to pursue that line. When it comes to motives, Barber, the picture broadens.'

'Yes, sir. When Mrs Channing is better she may let something slip,' replied Barber. 'Do we know when her husband is likely to be moved?'

Truscott got up.

'I think it'll be soon, could be this afternoon. Keep in touch with them and let me know which ward he's admitted to at Croydon General. If her husband feels better, Mrs Channing will go home. Leave it for a day or so before interviewing her. Get on with your other enquiries. I'll take care of Channing, all right?'

Barber nodded and felt better when Truscott left. He went back to his coffee and thumbed through the statements taken. He still had six others to do and started to make appointments over the phone. One of these was to Albert Squires, the vicar's ally and member of the parish council. Squires had been at the White Hart for a brief spell during Channing's visit and agreed to Barber calling at his home later in the afternoon. The last call Barber made was to the hospital. Channing was not to be moved to Croydon until 9 am the next day. He took the particulars and went to lunch.

Barber kept his appointment with Squires at the agreed time. He was offered a glass of beer but settled for a cup of tea. Squires opened a can of best bitter and settled back in his armchair.

'Bad business, this. From what I've heard, somebody nearly put Channing's light out.'

Barber had his notebook ready.

'Yes, he's had a bad time. Tell me, can you remember any strange faces in the Hart that night? I know most of the punch-up artists in the manor and they all have cast iron alibis.'

Squires said there were a few strangers in but they were young couples enjoying eachothers' company. He thought Channing looked depressed that night and made no attempt to talk to anyone.

'Ever heard talk about interviews with people re the war?' asked Barber.

'I know our vicar was having trouble with a few on the parish council,' said Squires.

'Do you mind telling me who these people were?' asked Barber.

'They're all elderly,' replied Squires, 'hardly in the punch-up bracket. Too many memories of the war here and not keen on the vicar's plan to get pally with the Germans. A lot of folk in Tallingwood feel that way, I'm afraid.'

'Yes,' said Barber. 'All right, we'll forget the council for a moment. What about chat over a few beers among the younger generation? Any strong views expressed there?'

Squires knew then that Barber had done some sniffing at the vicarage.

'Only a bit of bravado, I reckon. Been watching too many war films. Nothing really serious in my book.'

Barber persisted.

'Maybe, but I want to know what sort of bravado it was, Mr Squires, and above all, who indulged in it?'

Squires looked uneasy,

'Oh, it was only young Tommy Lake, captain of our darts team down at the Red Lion. He just said he thought Channing ought to be careful, that's all.'

Barber made a quick note.

'Do you think Lake was referring to the risk of violence?'

Squires didn't like the way things were going at all.

'I doubt it. Tommy's not that sort of lad. He was probably thinking of the unpopularity that Channing was going to suffer.'

Barber made another note.

'Just one more question; did Lake describe Channing as a Kraut lover?'

Squires was cornered.

'Yes he did, but a lot of people use that expression around here. I've even heard it used about the vicar! Do you want the names of every Tom, Dick and Harriet in Tallingwood?'

Barber folded his notebook.

'No, Mr Squires. That won't be necessary, just yet. As you said, all this has been a bad business. We ought to explore every avenue, you know, and none of them very pleasant. I'm obliged to you for your help.'

Squires cooled down.

'How is Mr Channing? Our vicar will want to know, I think.'

Barber stood up to leave.

'Well, he's better. Being moved to Croydon General Hospital in the morning. They have better facilities there and his recuperation can be monitored by a specialist.'

'A specialist in what?' asked Squires.

'Concussion,' replied Barber. 'They have to be very careful with that.'

'Yes,' said Squires. 'Headaches and blurred vision, as I remember it from the war. Could be a long job, then?'

Barber turned to Squires in the hallway.

'Yes, I'm afraid it could be. Good day, Mr Squires.'

9

Dieter looked rather pleased with himself as he sat opposite me in my office. He held up two white cards.

'One for you and one for me,' he announced with his famous smile. 'To mark the fiftieth anniversary of Kleinerts Travel Agency – the company is holding a reception at its Düsseldorf offices on Friday next. These invitations have been issued by Frau Weber, and wait for it, bracket, Head of Personnel, unbracket!'

I was impressed.

'What time is this shindig?'

Dieter handed me my invitation.

'Well it says 6 to 8pm but it could go on longer. Need to watch the booze intake. When we Germans throw a party, Michael, the outcome can get out of hand.'

'Yes, I've noticed,' said I. 'I wonder what sort of reception we'll get, reception being the operative word.'

'I shouldn't worry' said Dieter, 'she wouldn't have sent these invitations without a genuine desire to meet us.'

I thought about this and still felt some apprehension.

'Think you'll get a pink chit from Lotte?'

Dieter put his invitation in his pocket.

'I don't see why not. She's gone along with everything so far. This could be the end of things, in which case, she ought to welcome it.'

'OK,' I said. 'Any RSVP needed?'

'No,' said Dieter. 'We'll just turn up at the gentlemanly hour of seven. Stand there looking helpless in the hope that a couple of wild birds will rescue us!'

I had to laugh.

'Ewalt, you are a bloody menace. What happens if Head of Personnel Weber gets uptight about the war?'

Dieter's smile widened.

'Leave that to me, Michael. I told her we were post-war generation. She can't hold us responsible for anything!'

'I hope you're right, Herr Hauptmann, otherwise we could be out of there before you get a chance to mingle with birds of any sort!'

Dieter chuckled.

'I've a strong feeling it's going to be OK. Inge Weber has had time to think things over. Have you still got Bennecker's Koblenz number?'

I confirmed this.

'Good,' said Dieter. 'My bet is she will want it. The circumstances of her brother's death were very much on her mind when we last spoke. There was something amiss between the Neumann sisters after the war when the Rot Kreuz wrote to them. The elder sister in Passau might hold the key to it. Trouble is, the Nun of Passau could be in the throes of a terminal illness.'

I was taken aback by this.

'Good Heavens, Dieter. You've done so much more here than I know about!'

Dieter's smile faded.

'Michael, old friend, let's go to Düsseldorf on Friday. I'll pick you up from the mess at 6.30pm. I'll ring you if I can't make it.'

With that he rose to leave. My phone rang and I waved to Dieter as he left. My caller was Wing Commander Aitken who wanted me to explain some 'anomalies' as he put it, concerning the Laarbruch case. I knew this would mean a tedious discussion in his office and agreed to call in. My colleague, George Bradley, raised an eyebrow.

'Courage, mon brave!' he said. 'There's nothing wrong with your average senior secretarial officer that a bullet between the eyes wouldn't cure.'

I was past caring by that time.

'Tut-tut, Officer Bradley' I said and, collecting some papers, swept out of the office in readiness for another major confrontation.

The rest of the week went by, albeit in a state of siege. I was thankful when Friday arrived. Dieter picked me up from the mess as arranged and we were soon on our way to Düsseldorf.

'Lotte says that if you don't sort out that redhead, you're

going to lose her!' muttered my old friend.

'For Heaven's sake, Dieter. I've more things on my mind than that. I haven't see Margaret for weeks. You know what staff work is like.'

Dieter did know what it was like.

'Let's relax, Michael, enjoy ourselves for a while. These are my people here, you know. Just be yourself. If you run into any real difficulties at Kleinerts, send up the usual distress rocket, OK?'

I said I would.

When we arrived the car park was full, so Dieter left the Taunus at a parking- meter, swearing to himself as he fed the slot with coins. We entered the main foyer of Kleinerts and our invitations were looked at by a stern looking man who looked like an ex-boxer and probably was. After a brief exchange in German between Dieter and the watchdog, we were directed up to the next floor. This was being used as the reception room, very large, full of people and noisy with the babble of chat. Assuming they were members of staff, I noticed the women present had changed out of working clothes into something a little more decorative, all except one. This lady still wore a dark two-piece business suit, with white blouse. She stood at the far end of the room in earnest conversation with two elderly, important looking men. Dieter was equally quick to spot her.

'See that one at the far end, Michael? Five will get you ten that's her! Surprise surprise, she's not as bad as I expected.'

I kept a straight face.

'So what do we do? Stand here like a couple of lemons until your wild birds turn up?'

Dieter took a deep breath and tried to look dashing.

'Don't look now, old cock, but here comes the first of them. A bit old for us, never mind. What is it you say – many a good tune played on an old fiddle!'

'Ewalt!' I whispered. 'Try and behave for Heaven's sake!'

The lady who approached us spoke to Dieter first. The German was rapid but I managed to make out she was Frau Weber's secretary. She beckoned to a waiter and we were soon holding glasses of hock. I raised my glass and muttered 'Prosit, madame.'

Old Fiddle smiled sweetly.

'It's all right Mr Kendrick, we all speak English here, but thank you for your toast anyway! Frau Weber won't be long. She has the president of the company with her at the moment. If you would care to follow me, I'll see that you are offered some "sustenance", is it?'

I liked Old Fiddle, she was a lady. Dieter and I stood at the buffet table nibbling our cocktail snacks trying not to look too bored. Suddenly, she appeared. Dark, two piece business suit stood between us with a twinkle in her eyes. She spoke English for my benefit, which was very good of her.

'I can tell the military at fifty metres' she began. 'I'm Inge Weber. So glad you were able to come.'

Dieter gave Inge a respectful bow. I just smiled.

'Very kind of you to invite us, Frau Weber. Quite a party you have here!'

Inge fixed me with a knowing look.

'Fifty years of Kleinerts, Mr Kendrick. Important anniversary. We were in business before the first war and we had quite a struggle to get back on our feet after the second. We've had a lot of help from the Americans, one way or another. Tell me, how do you like it here in Germany?'

I said I liked it a lot, which wasn't exactly true, but I thought it polite to say so. She then turned to Dieter and they chatted away in their own language for a while. I had a chance to study Inge Weber at close quarters. She was not typically German in appearance. Dark hair taken back in a chignon style. High cheek bones though, with very blue Konrad Adenauer shaped eyes, a little bit on the slant.

'Ah, there's Germany,' I thought.

Always difficult to guess a woman's age but, in her case she looked to be in her mid-thirties. Dieter was making her laugh and she seemed to be enjoying his company. Most women did. I started to look around taking stock of everyone there. Mixed age groups with about equal numbers of men and women. Several languages were being used. French, Italian, Dutch and a few others I couldn't identify. Inge Weber must have realised I felt a bit out of things.

'Well, Mr Kendrick, it was most kind of your pastor to take an interest in my brother's grave. Kind of you too. I must write a letter of thanks in due course. You must let me have the pastor's name and address. When do you think you'll be going

77

home again?'

I had to admire her English; it was excellent and, like Dieter's, bore a slight American inflection.

'Not until the middle of September, Frau Weber, provided I can get away from my desk.'

She smiled at this.

'Yes, Herr Ewalt was telling me about that. Flying men seldom take kindly to desk jobs. You must be like a couple of caged tigers.'

It was my turn to laugh.

'More like a couple of rebellious pussy cats. Too many senior officers about at HQ to be anything else.'

Inge liked that answer and Dieter said something in German that made her laugh again.

'Come along, then' she said, 'let me introduce you around.'

Putting on a brave front we followed her.

Dieter and I spent the next half hour chatting to a number of the guests, all of whom seemed rather in awe of Inge. It was the usual cocktail party prattle. Nothing very profound. One lady, however, an American, was more direct than the others. When Inge introduced us, this lady raised her eyebrows.

'Well, Inge! Aren't you the sly one,' she trilled. 'You never told me you had friends in the military, such nice looking ones too.'

Dieter beamed, Inge frowned just for a second, and I stood there feeling uncomfortable. After the usual exchanges, Dieter and Mother America got down to some serious chat about the recent Cuban crisis. The husband of this lady was with the State Department, doing his stint in Bonn. As if reading my thoughts, Inge smiled at me.

'Don't take Connie too seriously, Mr Kendrick. She likes to tease and say outrageous things. She's a good friend of mine and looked after me so well during my two years in the States.'

'That explains the accent,' I thought.

'I envy you, Frau Weber. Never been to America. Maybe one day I will. What part of the States were you?'

Inge thought for a moment.

'New York at first. Now there's a town! After that, Washington. Not so much fun but good for business. Before I came back to Germany I did the usual tour, California, Texas, the Rockies. What would you like to see if you ever got there?'

78

'Hollywood,' I replied. 'Tinsel Town and the land of Bally-Hoo!'

Inge fixed me with those blue eyes of hers.

'You surprise me, Mr Kendrick, I would have thought something more serious would have drawn you.'

'Well, I'm not quite as serious as I look. Working with Ewalt here knocks all that out of me. I hope he hasn't been too presumptuous.'

'Oh no, Mr Kendrick,' said Inge, pretending to look severe. 'I wouldn't permit it!'

Then we both laughed.

'Herr Ewalt tells me you were good enough to do some research which would be of interest to me. We never knew the circumstances of our brother's death,' she said suddenly.

'That's so,' I replied, determined to get things right. 'Does the name Bennecker mean anything to you? Hugo Bennecker?' It didn't, so I continued. 'He flew with your brother, Frau Weber. They were trained together and served in the same unit in France. Both Dieter Ewalt and I met Herr Bennecker in Koblenz recently. I have his address and phone number with me, if you would like to take it.'

Inge said she would and taking out Bennecker's trade card, I handed it to her.

'I'm sure he would be pleased to meet you,' I added. 'He was fond of your brother. He will tell you everything.'

She looked so sad for just a fleeting moment.

'Yes I'm sure he will, Mr Kendrick. I was only a girl of fourteen when Kurt was killed. A long time ago I know. There was a great deal of anger and bitterness in my heart over things for almost ten years. Nearly all directed at your service, the RAF. I'm glad to say that time has healed the wound. Time always does.'

I hadn't the faintest idea what to say to that so I offered Inge a cigarette, which she accepted with a rather trembling hand. As I offered her a light, another thought came to mind.

'When you feel you would like to, Frau Weber, please ring me at Rheindahlen. Here is my number and extension there. The vicar of our church at home will be pleased that we have met. I will, of course, give you his address when the time is right.'

Inge nodded.

'Yes. I'm not quite sure when that will be. I have to go down to Bavaria shortly. My elder sister lives there and is not at all well.'

As an afterthought I then said, 'The Soldaten Friedhof people are re-interring the war graves next year. I'm not sure when this will be, but our vicar said he had heard from our own War Graves Commission. They are all being laid to rest at a place called Cannock Chase, Staffordshire – that's in the Midlands.'

'Yes,' said Inge. 'I have heard that too. For my part, I'd like to visit the grave in its present location. I can't speak for my sister, of course. If I did visit, I would try to combine it with a business trip to London. This place in Tallingwood is not that far off, is it?'

I said it wasn't, adding she could get there on a suburban line train in about thirty minutes.

'Our vicar will give you all the information you need, Frau Weber.'

'Thank you, Mr Kendrick,' she said. 'You've been very helpful and above all, most kind.'

Dieter had managed to get away from American Connie by now. She had sailed off in another direction to greet a latecomer to the party.

'I hope this officer is behaving himself,' said Dieter to Inge in English. 'He's a wily old bachelor, you know. Not a family man like me.'

'Yes I can tell,' said Inge. 'He hasn't got that hen-pecked look yet.'

Dieter tried to look hurt as Inge continued.

'Tell me about your children, Herr Ewalt. How many?'

Dieter brightened.

'Heidi is seven and Helga is five. Although Michael here calls them scalliwags, he spoils them dreadfully.'

Inge grinned and glanced in my direction.

'Ah, so there is hope for him yet! Beginning to show some parental instincts you think?'

Before Dieter could make some witty rejoinder at my expense, I chimed in quickly.

'Both Heidi and Helga are natural flirts. It's hereditary, I'm afraid.'

Dieter coughed and Inge chuckled.

'Will you fly again after Rheindahlen duties?'

Dieter answered first.

'Yes, I'm supposed to be going back on F-104s, as soon as Personnel find me a replacement.'

Turning to me, Inge offered a cigarette.

'What about you, Mr Kendrick?'

I lit up and said my piece.

'Well, they can't keep us in sackcloth and ashes for ever. I'm due for a flying tour next year. My CO seems to think it will be something large next time. That will mean a full tour as a co-pilot, I suppose. Twiddling the thrust levers and being allowed to raise and lower the undercarriage for some crusty old captain.'

Inge wanted to know more.

'You will have a large crew to consider, I expect. Does that worry you?'

I got the distinct feeling I was being analysed and then answered, 'You get used to flying on your own. Making your own decisions in a single seat. Being called to account for other people's errors and omissions is certainly a responsibility. I suppose at my age I should be ready for it.'

Inge thought about this before answering.

'It's a matter of progression, surely? To be in command of a big plane must demand a lot. Who knows, when they make you a crusty old captain one day, you might actually enjoy it.'

I had to smile at that.

'I certainly hope so,' was all I managed to reply.

Inge caught somebody's eye across the room and then turned to us.

'Our president is about to make his annual speech. If you'll excuse me, gentlemen, I have to introduce him.'

As she left us a waitress offered us recharged glasses and Dieter said, 'This will be for the toasts. Keep some fuel in reserve, Michael. Hope the old boy doesn't go on for too long or I might have a jettison problem.'

'Shouldn't drink so much,' I muttered. 'Hey, this is champagne.'

The room suddenly hushed as Inge Weber stood at the far end again. She stepped forward and gently tapped her wine glass with a spoon to attract attention. From that moment on, everything was in German. She spoke for about two minutes and then the president came forward. His address was mercifully short. It raised a few laughs and when concluded earned some polite applause.

'Thank goodness,' said Dieter. 'I'll be back in a minute. Don't get carried off by any amorous matrons!'

Inge still stood chatting to her president but her secretary came over for a brief word.

'It's Mr Kendrick, isn't it? I'm Hannelore Kietzmann. Hope you are not too bored by all this?'

I said I wasn't and added, 'This makes a nice change from the usual military get togethers. Most interesting and enjoyable, as a matter of fact. Thank you again for rescuing us when we arrived, Frau Kietzmann.'

She wore a wedding ring and looked to be in her fifties.

'Oh, that's all right' she said. 'I enjoy this sort of thing. Frau Weber was anxious that both of you should be greeted properly on arrival. Being tied up with our top management, she couldn't do it herself. That's the sort of delegation I like.'

I offered Frau Kietzmann, alias Old Fiddle, a cigarette but she declined.

'Does Frau Weber delegate a lot of things to you?' I asked with what I hoped was an engaging smile.

'Oh yes,' was the reply. 'Once Inge Weber gets to know and trust her staff, she lets them do far more than others I've worked for. Forgive me for asking, Mr Kendrick, but do you happen to know Father Heussinger of München Gladbach?'

I said I didn't.

'Oh, then it must be your friend, Hauptmann Ewalt, who put him on to us. He rang the other day.'

Hannelore Kietzmann paused.

'He came to see Frau Weber and was with her for quite some time. Ah! here is your friend.'

Dieter, now looking relieved, stood grinning at us.

'Everything in this place is most impressive, including the little boys room.'

Hannelore giggled.

'I'm sure Frau Weber would be most gratified to hear that.'

I thought it was about time Messers Ewalt and Kendrick went home before any more clangers were dropped. I needn't have worried. Dieter soon had Hannelore in stitches with some comments in German on the subject of Toiletten in general and his impressions of same world-wide, in particular. Before things got completely out of hand I was pleased when Inge Weber hove into sight again. She rejoined our little group and spoke to me first.

'I can see Hanne is looking after you well! Were you able to understand our president's speech, Mr Kendrick?'

I had to be honest with her.

'Not everything, I'm afraid, but I got the message about better understandings between Europeans all right. Good for business, I'm sure!'

'Ouch' said Inge. 'You don't pull your punches, Mr Kendrick. Perhaps what I said about your RAF was, well, what shall I say?'

'You don't have to apologise about that at all,' I replied. 'I can understand only too well how you must have felt in 1940. The main thing is, that I've enjoyed this evening and extremely glad that I came. Both Dieter and I would like to return your hospitality. Our favourite night-spot here is Karminski's. When you think the time is ripe for this, please get in touch.'

For the first time that evening, Inge Weber looked a little off balance.

'Yes, thank you,' she said. 'When I get back from Bavaria I would be pleased to do so.'

There followed a lengthy conversation in German between Dieter, Hannelore Kietzmann and Inge. We all shook hands. Dieter bowed and, doing the Continental thing, kissed the ladies' hands. I could see this made Hannelore's evening. We made our way down to the ground floor, past the ex-pugilist watchdog and out into the cool evening air. As Dieter and I boarded the Taunus in the alley way he opened up.

'That was a surprise, wasn't it, Michael?'

I had to agree that it was.

'She was very good. Much younger than I expected. Very sharp. Successful, confident, if a bit challenging. I had to bite my tongue a couple of times. Despite all that, I liked her.'

Dieter turned the ignition key.

'Uh-huh,' he said. 'Not the sort of woman it would be easy to get to know. Like Uhlbracht in Salmisch, she's cagey, cautious or what have you. On a purely physical level – she wasn't in my view, unattractive! Interesting bone structure, and those eyes!'

'Ewalt,' I sighed, 'does every woman have to fall into physical categories for you?'

Dieter chortled.

'Of course, what else is there in life?'

When I had finished chuckling, I turned to him as we left the alley way.

'You'd better play down the interesting bone structure and "those eyes" when you get home. Lotte will want to know all about this evening. Get too descriptive and she will eat the pair of us!'

Dieter was undeterred.

'Fear not, all will be well. The best thing that could happen is for Lotte to meet Inge Weber. We might be able to work on that sometime.'

'Let's get her back from Passau first,' I replied. 'She could be away for quite a time. Old Fiddle told me about a visit from a Father Heussinger last week. As a result of that call, she's high tailing it to Bavaria. Was that some of your handiwork?'

Dieter glanced at me quickly.

'Yes, in a round about sort of way. It might be a good thing, that visit. We could find out a lot more about those sisters. Wonder what it was that caused the rift between them?'

'Rift?' I asked. 'You never mentioned that before!'

'Oh sorry,' Dieter said breezily. 'I thought I had. It could have a bearing on no visits to your Tallingwood, Michael.'

I considered this.

'Even if it was, do you think Inge Weber is the type of person to tell us about it?'

'Probably not,' said Dieter, 'that's why I'd like her to meet Lotte. If they hit it off well and I think they would, Lotte would get it out of her!'

I had no doubt about that at all.

While Dieter and I were driving back to Rheindahlen, the Kleinerts' party was being tidied up. Most of the chores had been done and the ladies involved had a chance to unwind. Inge Weber and Hannelore Keitzmann sat sipping black coffee together.

'Come on, Hanne,' said Inge. 'What did you think of my

guests from Rheindahlen – out with it!'

'They made a good double act. Our own comedian and his British straight man. Ewalt was very funny, the complete extrovert. Kendrick has a lot of natural reserve, I think. To be fair, the language barrier must have been at the root of that. All the same, he could have been a little nervous.'

Inge nodded.

'Yes. That made two of us, then. I think we both knew it was going to be a difficult meeting. A certain amount of sparring on both sides. The points were about even, I'd say.'

Hannelore smiled.

'Not an easy people to get to know, let alone understand, our British cousins! When do you think you'll be going to Passau?'

Inge wasn't sure.

'It will need to be soon. Trudi's not well. I ought to make that trip next week if I can. I'll ring our München office on Monday, borrow one of our cars and drive to the convent. When I know the exact dates, I'll ring the mother superior in Passau. I'll leave you all the contact numbers before I go. The quickest way would be to take an internal Lufthansa flight from here to München. I'd expect to be away for a few days, that's all, Hanne. Don't look so worried! You can handle my job in your sleep.'

Hannelore Kietzmann knew that was true but liked to hear it said nevertheless.

'I can make some bookings for you on Monday when you finalise matters. We shouldn't have any real business problems for a while. The president looked pleased with things tonight.'

'Yes,' said Inge. 'So he should. Our trade figures are better than ever. Want a lift home?'

Hannelore accepted the offer with thanks.

10

The Monday following the Kleinerts' party I was late getting to the mess for lunch. Groupie had us all in his office until nearly 1 pm in another interminable round of brainpicking. As we were let off the leash, my colleague George Bradley turned to me in the corridor.

'Remember, Officer Kendrick, all good managers feed on their executives!'

'In that case,' I retorted, 'ours must be a bloody expert!'

When we got to the mess I checked the mail rack and found one letter for me bearing a Tallingwood post mark. The handwriting was unfamiliar and had been posted in the middle of the previous week. I opened it up and read it before going into lunch:

> 'Dear Mr Kendrick,
>
> I am writing to you at the request of Mrs Heather Channing. Her husband was admitted to Croydon General Hospital on the 10th, having sustained injuries in a vicious attack on the night of the 7th. Although Mr Channing is recovering slowly from his superficial injuries, he is still badly concussed. Mrs Channing is far too upset to write to you herself but felt you should be informed without further delay. She was aware you were in correspondence with her husband regarding some enquiries in Germany. For my part, knowing what those enquiries were, I have tried to establish the background of the assault on Mr Channing, so far without success. The Police believe the motive for the attack was robbery. His wallet and wrist watch were stolen. There are, however, reasons to suspect that Mr Channing may have been assaulted for taking such a

keen interest in our German war grave here. I am told his enquiries were most persistent and might have antagonised some with long memories of the war. I pray to God this will not prove to be the case as I would bear a strong sense of personal guilt for what has happened. If there is any further news regarding Mr Channing, I will write to you again.

Yours sincerely,
John Latimer
Rector of St Michael and All Saints, Tallingwood.'

I folded the letter and felt sick at heart. Skipping lunch, I went and had a coffee in the ante-room instead. What I really wanted to do was to take some leave, get home quickly and see Paul Channing. This was going to be difficult. The first thing to be done was to thank the vicar for his letter and then drop Heather a line. Just as I was thinking about all this Margaret McKinnon sat beside me, balancing her coffee cup on her knee.

'Hello, Mike! You're looking a wee bit glum!'

I told her about the letter and she listened sympathetically enough.

'An awful lot of this sort of thing going on these days,' she said. 'You don't think your friend being a journalist had anything to do with it?'

I said, 'Well, I know they are not the most popular of species, Margaret, but in his case he only runs the local rag. Nothing provocative or sensational in that.'

Margaret thought it prudent to change the subject.

'How are the Ewalts?'

I said they were fine and told her about Lotte's plot to get us on the Rhine boat trip. Margaret said she would be pleased to join us any time Lotte could fix it. She glanced at her watch.

'Sorry Mike, I've got to dash. See you.'

While this was going on in Rheindahlen, Inge Weber had rung Hugo Bennecker in Koblenz. She explained to him about our meeting and that she was planning a trip to visit her sister in Passau. She asked Bennecker outright if he was able to recall the circumstances of her brother's death in 1940. He said it would be better if the matter was discussed at a personal meeting between them. He suggested they met in Cologne, if that would be convenient. He was attending a motor trade conference there on Wednesday. The venue for this was going to be at the Dom Hotel, opposite the cathedral. He would be staying the night there and would be pleased to invite Inge to dinner at 8 pm if she could manage it. She consulted her diary and agreed. Bennecker told her to ask for him at Reception on arrival. She thanked him and, replacing the receiver, turned to the office intercom.

'Hanne, I've got to go down to Cologne on Wednesday evening. There's some information there I need before the Passau trip. As soon as I've got it, I'll ring the convent and suggest a visit on Friday. I'll probably be there over the weekend. Could you make that Lufthansa booking for Friday, please? I'll ring our Munich office now and make some preliminary arrangements.'

Hannelore had made a few notes.

'Yes Frau Weber. I'll do that. Any idea what day you'll be coming back?'

Inge didn't know and said she would get Kleinerts–Munich to fix the Lufthansa return, adding that she would ring her when she had a better idea of how things were.

And so, Wednesday evening came and Inge took the auto-bahn route to Cologne. She duly arrived at the Dom Hotel just after eight and didn't have long to wait at reception before Hugo Bennecker appeared. Looking very dapper in a blue pin-striped suit, he stepped forward.

'Good evening Frau Weber. I trust you had a trouble-free drive from Düsseldorf?'

Inge smiled.

'Yes thank you, Herr Bennecker. Did you have a good conference?'

He said it was interesting and a few useful leads had come his way.

'I'm a little out of practice entertaining ladies,' he added with a self-conscious grin. 'I hope I get things right!'

Inge took an instant liking to Hugo. He had the advantage of being an older man, which Inge always found the more interesting.

'This is a beautiful hotel,' she replied. 'I don't think you should have any trouble at all!'

Hugo suggested an aperitif but Inge preferred to dine straight away. They entered the dining room, which was fairly full already. The head waiter ushered them to a table near a large window overlooking the floodlit cathedral. The menu was produced, choices made and Hugo opened the proceedings.

'It was quite a surprise when those two young pilots were put on to me. I did enjoy their visit. Fine boys, both of them. They brought back so many memories of my younger days to me. I do so wish this meeting could have been under happier circumstances, Frau Weber.'

Inge, indulging in her usual act of analysis, suspected Hugo of being a lonely man. It didn't take her long to find out why. He had lost his wife five years ago, a victim of cancer. As a form of therapy, he had put all his energies into his work and done well financially. This had a familiar ring to Inge. She had done exactly the same when Franz Weber had died.

'My sister Trudi in Bavaria is a Carmelite nun. She too has a terminal carcinoma. I have to fly down there on Friday and want to make my peace with her before the end. I won't go into the whys and wherefores of things, but we have been estranged for many years. Most of it hinged upon our brother Kurt. The rest of it was over religious differences. I'm not a good Catholic, you see.'

Hugo sensed a far greater conflict between the sisters than Inge was ready to admit.

'She will want to know how her brother died, I think,' he said.

'Yes' said Inge. 'The young pilots said that you would be able to help us.'

Hugo replied that he would tell Inge as much as he could remember and suggested this be done over coffee after dinner. Inge understood and although only toying with her meal, was glad that her host seemed to enjoy his. They both declined a dessert and the coffee was produced without delay. Hugo told Inge about his friendship with her brother at Werneuchen and when it came to events in France he offered her a cigarette, which she accepted. As he described the raid on England on 9 September, Inge opened her handbag and dabbed her eyes with a handkerchief taken from within. Hugo placed his hand across the table and laid it upon Inge's.

'It was, in my opinion, over within seconds. Your brother was gone, Frau Weber, long before there could have been any suffering. Tell your sister that when you see her. For God is my judge, I believe this to be the truth!'

At this point, Hugo beckoned to the waiter and asked Inge if she would care to join him in a brandy. She accepted.

'How strong the family resemblence is,' he remarked. 'You are so like Kurt. Not only in appearance but in temperament also. It's been like talking to him again after all these years.'

Inge gripped Hugo's hand across the table.

'We owe these young pilots something, I think. Not an easy thing for the Englishman to have done. When we met he said something which has haunted me ever since. I was silly and emotional and told him of my anger and bitterness about everything. I shouldn't have done that. Anyway, he said he understood only too well how I felt in 1940. There was some event for him – in those days. I feel this most strongly.'

Hugo sipped his brandy.

'Will you see the Englishman again? If you do, give him my regards, I liked him.'

Inge told Hugo then about her plan to visit England and mentioned my willingness to help her in Surrey.

'I would like to go across,' said Hugo. 'I've been thinking about doing this for some time. If we can lay the Englishman's ghosts to rest, Frau Weber, who knows? He might be willing to help me as well?'

Inge nodded and smiled.

'I'm sure he will, Herr Bennecker! I'll mention it to him when next we meet. Forgive me, it's late. I don't want to run into fog on the autobahn. Thank you for inviting me here this evening. You have been the perfect host! I don't think you are out of practice at all.'

Hugo looked pleased.

'If ever business brings you down to Koblenz, Frau Weber, I'd be honoured to do this again.'

He smiled rather sadly, as if suspecting this would be the last he would ever see of her. They took their leave of one another at the hotel entrance. Inge fumbled for the car keys in her handbag. When she finally found them she extended a hand. Hugo gave a polite bow and raised Inge's hand to his lips – very briefly.

'Aufwiedersehn, Inge Weber. I wish you a safe journey to Bavaria.'

Inge nodded and smiled.

'Aufwiedersehn, Hugo Bennecker, and thank you for everything.'

With that she was gone. He suddenly felt old and tired. As he strolled towards the lift to return to his room, he wondered what Inge Weber had thought of him. 'No fool like an old fool,' he thought to himself.

Inge's drive back to Düsseldorf was uneventful. When she arrived at her flat she put some coffee on. It was already late but she didn't feel tired. Tomorrow she would ring the convent in Passau. 'What on earth do I tell Trudi?' she thought. 'Poor Hugo Bennecker. It must have been hard for him tonight. He handled things so well, I must try and make it up to him some day. I wonder if he's right about laying Kendrick's ghosts to rest? There must be a lot of ghosts on both sides to be rested. Even after all these years.'

On the following day Inge rang the convent and was told her sister was rallying a little but still weak. A room would be made available for her as long as Inge needed it. Her next call was to Kleinerts in Munich. When they knew who was calling, nothing was too much trouble. Hanne Kietzmann had booked the Lufthansa flight for Friday morning and all arrangements were completed. And so it was that Inge Weber found herself aboard that short-haul Boeing bound for Munich that Friday.

It was a bright clear day and on the flight down, Inge started to look back into the past. Looking back. Thinking back. That little chalet home in Salmisch – 1938. Her brother Kurt had been accepted for pilot training in the new Luftwaffe that summer. He had dreamed of nothing else since he was a boy. As a twelve year old girl then, Inge adored her brother who, despite the ten years that separated them, still had time for her. They appreciated the same things and laughed a lot together in those days. When Kurt had joined the Hitler Youth Movement, the main attraction being gliding, Inge had entered the Hitler Madel. Elder sister Trudi had protested at Kurt's and Inge's lack of church attendances and the beginnings of the rift had started. When their mother, who had never been very strong, suffered the first of her heart attacks, Kurt was already at recruit school in Landsberg. When the final blow fell and the

91

doctor advised the Neumann family that she had only a short time to live, Kurt was given seven days' leave. His mother lingered on and when he applied for an extension of leave, this was refused. It was late September 1938 and the Munich crisis over Czechoslovakia put all units of the German armed forces on full alert. Trudi Neumann could not understand the seriousness of all this and blamed her younger brother for not making a stronger case in applying for further leave. Within days of Kurt's return to his unit his mother had gone. When he was unable to get leave to attend his mother's funeral, it was too much for Trudi. She felt that her brother did not care enough. His military life came first and some terrible exchanges occurred over the phone and by letter. Inge had taken her brother's side but was dismissed as an atheist by Trudi. Endless arguments followed, in which Inge, in her turn, dismissed the Catholic Church. She horrified Trudi by describing the church as creepy and medieval. Quite apart from the boring rituals, what right did anyone have to listen to the secrets of a young girl's innermost soul? Inge hated the confessional and, in one terrible scene, threw her rosary to the floor. Trudi retrieved it, sat down and wept.

Throughout all this, Papa Alfred Neumann remained silent. As an old soldier he knew full well his son's position. Nevertheless, he understood how Trudi felt and, taking after her mother in religious fervour, preferred not to take issue with her. He had troubles enough now that his wife had died. He had to admit that Inge was beginning to be a problem. Ruefully, he wished he'd had a family of sons. Easier to understand in so many ways. Although loving his daughters, he found them neurotic at times, which made him weary.

Inge remembered all this and glanced out of the cabin window as Frankfurt passed below. 'How much longer to Munich?' she thought. '1946 was a bad year. Dear God, it was a terrible year.'

She closed her eyes and thought back again.

By the autumn of 1946, Papa Alfred Neumann had died. He had been ill for some time. It had begun with cancer of the prostate and had developed remorselessly into the stomach within a matter of a few months. Trudi had recently taken her vows at the convent and was given leave to attend her father's funeral. Inge felt she was further away from Trudi than she ever was. There were so many matters to be attended to now that Papa had gone. She asked Trudi about the sale of the chalet and other financial matters. With her vows of poverty, chastity and obedience, none of this made any impact upon Trudi at all. The rift seemed total. There was nothing between the sisters to hold them together. A few days after the funeral, Inge had to go to Passau and make arrangements with the solicitor, bank manager and the probate officer. She had a great deal to do. It was on this morning that the Red Cross letter arrived at Salmisch. Trudi opened it and read the contents. It said simply that Feldwebel K. Neumann had been buried in the Anglican church of St Michael and All Saints in Tallingwood, Surrey, England. A photograph of the grave was enclosed and any further communications were to be addressed to the Red Cross at Frankfurt. Trudi, in an emotionally disturbed state, tore up the letter and cast it into the fireplace. Without waiting for Inge's return she caught the bus from Salmisch to Passau. This was the last Trudi had seen of Inge for many years. Inge had called in to the convent when her husband Franz Weber had died, some years later. She knew full well what her sister Trudi had done with the Red Cross letter in 1946. She had found it a few days later in the fire grate at Salmisch, and felt so much bitterness ever since.

As Inge looked out of the aircraft window, down onto her native Bavaria, nearing Munich, she thought.

'I'm not a good Christian at all, least of all a Catholic. What can I say to Trudi? What can we women say to one another? It's been so many years since I have prayed: Hail Mary – full of Grace – the Lord is with Thee – blessed art thou amongst women – blessed is the fruit of thy womb, Jesus. Holy Mary, Mother of God, pray for us sinners, now and at the hour of our death, Amen.'

Inge had not remembered those words for so long. She knew there would be a great deal of prayer at the convent. Somehow, she had to go through with it all.

The Lufthansa air hostess suddenly looked down at Inge.

'Is everything all right?' she asked.

Inge managed to collect herself.

'Yes thank you, what time are we due at Munich?'

The hostess, realising she was being spoken to by a lady of authority, smiled politely.

'We shall be landing in five minutes. I hope you have had a pleasant flight.'

11

At about the same time that Inge Weber sat at her sister's bedside in Bavaria, Inspector Truscott was sitting at Paul Channing's bedside in a ward at the Croydon General Hospital. Paul was sitting up and appeared to Truscott to be sufficiently lucid to answer some questions.

'Mr Channing, the doctors say that I must not tire you. Tell me if I do. I can always come back another day.'

Paul raised a faint smile.

'That's all right. I'm still a bit dazed and sore. I suppose you want to go over everything, about how I come to be here?'

Truscott nodded.

'Let's start with why you were in the White Hart that night and drinking alone, shall we?'

Paul's smile faded.

'My word, you really have been doing your homework, haven't you. Who told you that?'

Truscott told Paul about DC Barber's enquiries and said it was all routine.

'If you were waiting for somebody, Mr Channing, you'd make my job easier if you told me who it was. A lady perhaps?'

'Cherchez la Femme, Inspector Maigret?'

Truscott didn't think that was very funny.

'Look, Mr Channing, you can treat what happened to you as a joke but I don't. Next time you may not be so lucky. If you were planning to meet a lady and a married one at that, I'd like to know about it. It cuts down on a list of suspects.'

Paul began to chuckle quietly.

'And points the finger at some jealous husband? How bloody convenient! No. Inspector, it was nothing like that at all. I'd received an anonymous note from somebody who claimed to know something about the Plover's Green case in 1940. I waited an hour but nobody approached me in the bar that night. So, feeling a bit fed up, I decided to go home.'

Truscott leaned forward.

'Why the detour to Tallingwood Grove?'

Paul frowned.

'Thinking about the war, I suppose, thought I'd go via the war memorial, that's all. I was perfectly sober and didn't hear them behind me – yes, that's right, there were two of them. Young, quick and very strong. I was able to elbow one of them in the ribs, good and hard. Could have broken something, as he really yelled. The other sod had a punch like a pile-driver and caught me off balance. All I can remember before I passed out was throwing a punch at Pile-driver that landed on his fat fleshy face. See this? His teeth took the skin of my knuckles. I think I dislodged a couple of his dentures; didn't find any, did you?'

Truscott sighed.

'No we didn't, he probably took them with him! We took a good look at the place in the morning. At least Barber did. All right, so you could have been mugged but I doubt it. Have you still got that anonymous note, Mr Channing?'

Paul thought for a moment.

'It's in my office drawer. It was hand written in block capitals, Miss Watkins, my secretary could probably find it.'

Truscott looked annoyed.

'Why on earth didn't you tell us about it before? Did you forget everything I told you when I called at your office? We could have been at the White Hart that night and saved all this!'

Paul looked truculent.

'You dismissed the Plover's Green story as a "legend", Inspector. You didn't want to believe it did you? You say now you doubt I was mugged, in which case, the "legend" could have been fact and this assault was my reward for asking too many questions. What say you to that?'

Truscott sat back in his chair before answering.

'It's the war memory that led to your assault. There is no evidence that we have to indicate that a German airman was murdered here in Tallingwood in 1940 and I'd be doing less than my duty if I did not tell you so.'

Paul began to look tired and Truscott could see it.

'Mr Channing, thank you for telling me what you have

done. It will be a lot of help. Would you mind if I called in again in a few days?'

Paul closed his eyes.

'If ever you catch that young bastard with his front teeth missing, remember he's mine. I want him – alone!'

'Hm,' muttered Truscott, 'we shall see about that, get some rest.'

With that he rose to leave. On his way out of the ward Inspector Truscott was confronted by a formidable looking ward sister who bore down on him with an awful suddeness.

'If you are Inspector Truscott of Croydon CID, Doctor Freeman wants a word with you.'

'So where is he?' challenged Truscott.

'Wait there!' said the formidable presence.

'Up yours,' muttered Truscott and the ward sister pretended not to hear.

When Doctor Freeman eventually appeared, he looked as harrassed as he had done in Tallingwood.

'Hello Inspector – Mr Channing's x-rays have just come in. I'm a little worried about them. There seem to be some odd marks here and there, which might be haemorrhaging. I hope you didn't spend too much time with him?'

'No, just a few minutes. He was very helpful and thanks for letting me see him. I'll need to speak to him again if that's possible?'

'Provided you can resist the temptation not to antagonise the nursing staff, Inspector, I think that might be arranged. I'll ring you when I think Channing is fit enough.'

Truscott shot a sideways glance at Freeman, nodded and left the ward.

When he got back to his office, Truscott put a call through to Barber at Tallingwood. He wanted to know if Barber had interviewed Mrs Heather Channing yet. He had. Barber, as usual, was on the defensive with Truscott.

'Not a lot to go on really, sir. Mrs Channing mentioned some RAF chum of her husband's. Name of Kendrick. A flight officer – pilot I think, serving in Germany.'

Truscott was going to enjoy this.

'For your information, Constable Barber, a flight officer is a female WAAF rank. Since when have women been pilots in the RAF?'

Barber was speechless for a moment.

'I could have got the rank wrong, sir; anyway, this Kendrick has been making some enquiries in Germany re the war grave here in Tallingwood. Seems this Kendrick's getting leave to come home and visit the Channings.'

Truscott had some alarm bells ringing in his head at that news.

'Did you find out how soon it would be, where Kendrick would be staying?'

'Yes, sir. He's a local man. His parents live at Woodlands Lane, number 11, The Gables, should be home by the weekend.'

Truscott tried hard not to sound impressed.

'All right lad, I'll interview Flight Lieutenant Kendrick. Any other leads?'

Barber swallowed.

'I've still two more to do, sir. Anything from Mr Channing?'

Truscott smiled maliciously on the other end of the line.

'All in good time, Barber, lad.'

'Yes, sir' was all Barber was able to mutter.

As Truscott replaced the receiver he wondered whether the time was ripe to ring London, and decided against it.

'Who the hell is this bod, Kendrick?' he mused. 'Talk about a festering intrigue, the Yard will go bananas at this one.'

A week before this, back in Germany, I showed the Reverend Latimer's letter to Groupie and told him all about events since my sister's wedding. He was surprisingly sympathetic, especially with my request for leave, albeit for only seven days. He peered at me over the top of his bi- focals.

'In the interests of Anglo-German relations, Kendrick, you can go home for a week but that's all. You're pretty pally with a boy from Luftwaffe Flight Safety – aren't you?'

I said that I was.

'Well,' said Groupie, 'if it's a question of tracing relatives in West Germany, that's one thing. I wouldn't want any complications which might embarrass us politically. I hope you understand what I'm getting at?'

I said that I did.

When I got back to my office, George Bradley looked up sharply from his desk.

'Hey, mate! You've just had a phone call.'

'Oh God,' I sighed. 'Not that old toad Aitken again?'

George shook his head.

'Oh, no. It was a lady. A Mrs Heather Channing from Blighty; said she'd ring back in an hour or so. Sounded a bit agitated, I thought.'

'Thanks George, any other business? I'm taking some leave at the weekend.'

'Nothing to get wound up about,' said my colleague. 'Just the usual stream of boring admin crap!'

I had to smile at that. George Bradley was enjoying his ground tour as much as I was enjoying mine. He was just waiting for the day those 'crooks' at the Air Secretary's branch posted him back to flying duties. I carried on for a while, sifting through the paperwork until my phone rang again. As I remember, the conversation ran as follows:

'Hello Mike, it's Heather.'

'Hello there. Sorry I was out when you rang earlier. How's Paul?'

'Oh, Mike. I'm worried sick. They want to operate on him. It will be soon, within the next few days. I've had a visit from the police. It's been awful.'

'OK, Heather, take it easy. I'm coming home. The vicar wrote and told me about everything. I'm flying over on Friday and will be with you first thing Saturday morning. Kids all right?'

'Upset about Paul, naturally, but being kids have no idea how serious things are.'

'Don't worry, Heather. Paul's in the best place. I'll call you when I get home. Try and get some rest now.'

'I just can't sleep Mike. Going over all the things I've said and done. Paul and I have been going through a very rough patch lately. Now all this. Oh Mike, help me.'

'Yes Heather, you can count on that. Just hang on.'

The line went dead as I said that and I felt completely useless. I don't know how I got through the rest of the working day. George must have overheard everything but said nothing. The third member of our office team, Freddie Flynn, suddenly appeared at the door.

'What's up with you two? Look like a couple of undertaker's mutes. Who's been at it this time? SASO, Groupie or bloody

99

Aitken?'

George Bradley was the first to reply.

'Officer Flynn! Get your butt into your chair and start earning your flying pay.'

Freddie raised an eyebrow.

'Charming! Out of the office for ten minutes and I find you lot looking like the tail end of a Greek tragedy!'

'It's all right Freddie' I said, 'George has had a bad day.'

'So what's new about that,' said Freddie. 'By the way, there's a buzz around the mess that your mate Ewalt has been posted to Oldenburg. Goes in the spring. Promoted to major, they reckon, when the time comes. Goes to command an F104 outfit. Poor sod! I wouldn't wish that even on Aitken.'

I certainly pricked my ears up at that.

'Thanks, Freddie. Nice to know that at least one of us here keeps his finger on the pulse.'

Freddie Flynn grinned.

'Oh, knickers! Kendrick. Flattery will get you anywhere.'

When I got back to the mess in the early evening, I put a call through to Dieter's married quarter. Lotte answered it.

'Hello, Lotte' I said. 'I've heard some disturbing rumours about your "gemahlen", like a posting in the spring! What's up, or is that a Federal Republic military secret?'

Lotte giggled.

'Michael Kendrick, you're impossible! Weren't you in the mess today? Hang on a minute, I'd better get Dieter on the line.' Then, as an afterthought, Lotte added, 'What's all this I hear about you going home to England this weekend?'

I thought about this for a second before answering.

'The trouble with you, Lotte is, you know too many wives of senior British officers on this base.'

There was a pause at this before Dieter came on the line.

'We had quite a party lunch time today, Mike. We all missed you! Will I see you before you leave for England? Your Groupie's wife told Lotte about that, lunch time today.'

I felt a bit annoyed.

'Bloody female bush-telegraph in action again. Can't you discipline your women in the new Germany, Ewalt?'

Dieter thought this amusing and started to laugh.

'Ever tried disciplining your own women, Michael?'

I had to admit, as a bachelor, I hadn't. Dieter wanted to

know why I had decided to take leave so suddenly. I told him about Paul Channing's 'mugging', his injuries and the need for the operation. I mentioned Heather Channing's phone call to me that morning.

'I'm sorry, Michael,' said Dieter. 'After all, he was the one that started you off, wasn't he?'

I hesitated for a moment.

'About the Neumann case, yes. That's right.'

Dieter wanted me to call in to his quarter tomorrow evening for a drink and a chat.

'I know you'll only be away for a week, Michael, but we ought to think about Frau Weber now. Lotte has agreed to invite her over for a meal one evening.'

I said I would call in after 8 pm, if that was all right. It was.

Over dinner, I started to think about Inge Weber and wondered how she was getting on in Bavaria. She would have a shock if she knew about Paul and the letter Padre Latimer had written to me. 'Getting Lotte Ewalt to invite Inge Weber must have taken some doing,' I thought.

Then I started to collect my thoughts about the Channings. Heather was obviously still in a state of shock. A bad business all round. The sooner I got back to Tallingwood the better. I wanted to call in on the Rev. Latimer when I got home. There were one or two questions I wanted to put to him.

The following evening, I sat chatting to Lotte and Dieter Ewalt. Dieter was full of his posting in the spring and I could see Lotte was pleased about the promotion.

'Dieter and I have thought things over, Michael, about Frau Weber,' said Lotte. 'Pity we couldn't invite her over before you go on leave. At least you'll have something to tell the pastor when you get back.'

I resisted the temptation to ask Lotte why she had changed her mind about the Neumann case.

'Yes, that's right,' I said, 'I think the old boy will be pleased.'

Dieter raised an eyebrow.

'Do you think he will be equally pleased if Hugo Bennecker visited the church?'

'I don't see why not,' I replied. 'He wants to put the war behind us. We don't have to put a notice in the parish magazine about Bennecker, do we?'

Dieter frowned.

'Is that an English joke, Michael?'

I tried to look contrite.

'Not exactly. All I meant was, we would need to be discreet about it – that's all.'

Lotte shot me a quick glance.

'As discreet as you have been over here, with us, Michael?'

'What on earth is that supposed to mean, Lotte dear?'

She took a deep breath before answering.

'Dieter dismisses the fact that women have a certain intuition. I've felt for some time, Michael, that there's something more in the Neumann case that you would prefer us not to know!'

Dieter grimaced at his wife.

'Oh Liebling! What a thing to suggest!'

I was at bay here and thought carefully before answering.

'At least we've got you talking about the war, Lotte. I was pleased when Dieter told me about the decision to invite Frau Weber over. There may be some more facts to emerge. There often are. It's not going to be easy for any of us. I've told you everything I can.'

Lotte looked me straight in the eye.

'And what about the things that you can't or won't?'

Dieter was beginning to look annoyed at his wife.

'Lotte, Michael is our good friend and our guest. I think we should change the subject.'

I felt uncomfortable and Lotte put her hand on mine.

'Sorry Michael, forgive me. Perhaps I'm just a silly woman after all. I'll put the coffee on.'

Dieter and I were left alone in the lounge and we chatted about the F104 posting in the spring. He knew it would be something of a challenge but felt relieved his ground tour was coming to an end. He asked about my future and I said it would depend on the choices I was offered. When Lotte rejoined us with the coffee she asked me what I had done with Margaret McKinnon.

'I think she's got a couple of ardent suitors over at Laarbruch.'

'Oh Michael,' said Lotte with a faint smile. 'You'll lose her if you're not careful. A girl likes to be pursued, you know. You're too casual, I think.'

Dieter laughed.

'He's just playing hard to get, it never fails. He's a wily old British buzzard, this one.'

We all laughed at that; it helped to relieve the earlier tension. Before I knew it, it was time to go. I had a lot to do. I hadn't even packed my things in readiness for the trip home to Tallingwood.

☆　　☆　　☆

The flight home was uneventful. After I had eaten one of Mother's gargantuan meals, I put a call through to Heather Channing. She told me that Paul had been operated on the day before. He seemed to have come through it well, according to Doctor Freeman at the hospital. I asked Heather about visiting hours.

'I'm going over tomorrow. What about you?'

'See how he is,' I replied. 'I'll call in at the hospital on Monday. In the meantime, can I pop round to see you this afternoon?'

'Yes, of course' said Heather. 'Come round for tea about 4.30.'

She sounded more relaxed, probably over the news from the hospital.

'OK, Heather. Thanks. I've got some things to do this morning. Look forward to seeing you.'

The next call I made was to Padre Latimer at the vicarage. He seemed pleased to hear from me, and when I said I had some information from Germany he asked me if I would be able to attend church service on Sunday.

'Yes, Padre. Could we have a chat afterwards?'

He suggested I took coffee with him at the vicarage after the service and I agreed. I had only been back in the lounge for a few minutes when the phone rang. I lifted the receiver.

'Good morning,' said an unfamiliar voice. 'My name is Truscott. Inspector Truscott of Croydon CID. Is Flight Lieutenant Kendrick at home. please?'

I said I was.

'Sorry to bother you, Mr Kendrick, I was wondering if it would be convenient for us to have a chat one day next week? I'm investigating the Channing case, you see. Channing's wife said you were home for a few days and, being a close friend of theirs, I thought you might be able to help us?'

I told Truscott about my planned visit to the hospital on Monday and suggested a meeting in Croydon.

'Fine,' said Truscott. 'Come around to the station when you are free. I shall be in all day. I'll tell the desk sergeant to expect you.'

With that he put the receiver down. He certainly sounded a brisk, business-like individual. Not one to waste words. I felt a bit intrigued at all this. Being interviewed by the police would be a novel experience. I wondered what he was after and above all, how he would go about it.

When I arrived at Heather Channing's she seemed genuinely pleased to see me.

'Oh Mike. It's so good of you to come over,' she said giving me a hug.

'That's all right Heather' I said. 'What about you and the children? Any problems apart from the obvious ones?'

Heather shrugged.

'If you mean financial, no. Paul's insurance takes care of that one. It's something else. The police have been here several times and made some nasty insinuations. A nurse down at the cottage hospital with a runaway mouth told them Paul and I were having marital problems.'

I nodded.

'Don't all couples have them, Heather?'

She thought carefully before answering.

'The police think Paul could have been attacked by some jealous husband. If he had been carrying on with some woman, I wouldn't blame him, I've been a bitch to Paul. The thought of nearly losing him has brought that home to me!'

'I can't see Paul having an affair with another woman,' I replied. 'It's not in his nature at all. Far more likely he was attacked for asking too many questions about the Plover's Green case during the Blitz.'

Heather placed her arms akimbo.

'Bloody Germans,' she snorted, 'all the trouble and misery they've caused the world. Why should Paul get so wrapped up in all this? Does it matter a damn how that German died?'

'It seems to matter a great deal to Paul, Heather. He just felt it was only the enemy that did that sort of thing.'

104

Heather would have none of this.

'Oh, the upright British sense of fair play and decency. Can't he see that all men are capable of cruelty and violence?'

'We don't even know that it happened,' I replied. 'Too long ago to prove anything. Paul's been on some personal crusade in search of the truth. Perhaps that's how he feels a journalist should behave, the better ones at any rate.'

Heather considered this and sighed.

'So what's been happening in Germany? Paul said you had found some relatives out there.'

I told her about Inge Weber and all the help from the Ewalts.

'Well,' said Heather, 'that doesn't help Paul does it? Something has got to be done to lay his obsession to rest.'

I had thought about this too.

'We need to prove conclusively to Paul that Neumann was in that plane when it crashed at Vernon Road. Some eye witness. Civil defence teams, fire service or police who must have been there and seen everything, unpleasant as it must have been. If we can find people like that, some of whom must still be living, we might be able to effect a "cure".'

Heather shook her head.

'That's precisely what Paul's been trying to do all these months. We can't start probing again, Mike. I don't want to see you laid up in Croydon General! When I said I needed your help, I really meant that Paul's more likely to listen to you than me. Please persuade him to give up this whole investigation before it destroys us all!'

She was right, of course.

'I'll certainly try,' I said. 'Now that we've located one of the sisters in Germany, he may feel he's done enough.'

Heather's eyes narrowed at this.

'Sister, you say. Must be getting on a bit, I suppose?'

'Quite young actually, in her thirties I'd say.'

'What's she like?'

'Successful business woman. My chum in the West German Air Force thinks she's rather attractive.'

'Hm' said Heather, 'beauty is as beauty does. Up to her pretty neck with the Nazis during the war no doubt!'

I smiled at this.

'No doubt. They all were in one way or another. They went

along with Hitler for what they thought they could get out of it. It's a delicate subject though, and if ever she visits her brother's grave, some people here are going to have to make an effort to put this out of mind.'

'Like the vicar' said Heather. 'All right for him and his Christian virtues. If some of his parishioners hear about this, his church is going to be even emptier than it is at present.'

'Yes, you may well be right. I've got an appointment to see him tomorrow, after the service.'

'Well, he started all this. Let's see if he can finish it. I'll put the tea on now.'

I sat in the lounge, admiring the Channings' garden. Such a peaceful scene. So well kept. When Heather returned with the tea, we sat chatting about life in Tallingwood, old friends and the new estates springing up like mushrooms in the area. When it was time to go, Heather gave me a peck on the cheek. I said I would ring her on Sunday evening. Just to find out how Paul was. I didn't mention my visit to the Croydon CID on the Monday. 'One thing at a time,' I thought.

On the following morning I went to St Michael's and All Saints church. It was a family service and surprisingly well attended. Padre Latimer's sermon rambled on a bit. Some of the children were bored and restive. When it was over I stood by the old Norman arch and waited for Latimer.

'Hello, Mr Kendrick, how good it is to see you,' he said shaking my hand firmly.

'Good morning, Padre. I forgot to thank you for the letter when I rang.'

'Oh that's all right. Poor Mrs Channing. She was in such a state. Have you had a chance to see her?'

'Yes, yesterday. Her husband's had the operation and she seems more relaxed about things.'

'Thank heavens. Let's hope and pray he makes a full recovery.'

'Amen to that. I'm going over to Croydon to see him tomorrow, provided he's well enough.'

'Give our warmest regards and best wishes to him.'

'Of course. I was wondering if we could have a chat about the war grave?'

Latimer looked resigned.

'As long as it doesn't involve any more enquiries here. I

understand from Mr Channing, before this dreadful business, that you had actually found some relatives.'

'That's right. I think one of them may come over for a visit.'

I told Latimer about Inge Weber then as we strolled slowly towards the vicarage. When we arrived there the coffee was put on. The study had an extensive library and I wondered whether Latimer ever had the time to read everything there. We sat by the French windows overlooking the lawn and continued our conversation.

'So, they are Catholics then,' said Latimer.

'Not as staunch as some. I got the impression that Frau Weber wasn't as devout as her sister.'

'That's the Carmelite, you say. Well they don't come any more devout than that.'

'Well, we're not likely to see her here. She has a terminal illness.'

'Oh dear. How I wish there could be some movement towards church unity. Perhaps one day it will come. So much would depend upon the Vatican, although I don't see it in my lifetime!'

'There's somebody else who may come over with Frau Weber. Name of Bennecker. He flew with Neumann on that last raid. Not in the same plane, he was the pilot of another. Would Christian forgiveness stretch that far, Padre?'

'That, Mr Kendrick, stretches beyond all human understanding. I would welcome Herr Bennecker but I'm not sure many of my parishioners would!'

'Yes, talking of them, what made you feel Paul Channing was attacked because of the war?'

'Oh, some general comments. Nothing I would care to repeat. The police have looked into all that.'

'Any idea when the grave is being moved to Staffordshire?'

'Next summer, I believe. It's going to be a long job. Tell me, you must have had a struggle with your own conscience coming to terms with the New Germany.'

'In what way?'

'Your school friends. The Lindsays. You were going to tell me about them.'

'I was very fond of them and their mother. It was a terrible shock to us all. Time has healed the wounds, as it always does. As I grew up, perhaps I realised that hate was the self-destructive force they said it was.'

'Yes. It warms my heart to hear you say that. From what I've been told, the new Germans understand well enough how the rest of the world feels about them. Perhaps what they don't realise yet is that as long as the generation that fought the war lives long enough to remember it, few will forgive them. And yet, the Germans have to go on with life, wondering if they can ever be accepted by the rest of the human family.'

'Well they can't do that alone. Some of us have made a start, as hard as it may seem. I was lucky with the Ewalts. I never thought I could get so close to two people and a German couple at that!'

'Do you believe in Providence, Michael?'

That was the first time Padre Latimer had called me that.

'Like Dunkirk and the Battles of Britain and the Atlantic?'

'Maybe, but I had something else in mind. Closer to home for you. Was your friendship with the Ewalts predestined in some way?'

'Now you've got me out of my depth, Padre. I'm not a student of theology.'

Latimer smiled.

'I think you only pretend to be flippant. From what you've told me already, I know there's a Christian there somewhere! Forgive me. I think you've had enough sermons for one day.'

We both laughed at that. I finished my coffee and said I should be getting home. My mother would fret if her lunch was spoiled. Latimer saw me to the vicarage gates.

'Tell Frau Weber and Herr Bennecker I will be pleased to receive them – any time. As long as I know when to expect them.'

I said I would see this was done and thanked him for everything. On the way home I felt relieved that the good padre had made no reference to the real nature of Paul Channing's enquiries. Surely by now he must have heard about the Plover's Green case, yet he made no mention of it. Was he still in ignorance?

That evening, I rang Heather Channing and she said Paul was very drowsy during the visit. They only let her stay for ten minutes. Offering to put off my visit for a day or two, Heather insisted I went as planned.

'He's looking forward so much to seeing you, Mike. Don't

disappoint him. How was church and the vicar this morning?'

'Very good, thank you. Good for the soul too!'

Heather chuckled.

'Not before time either. Give me a call when you can.'

'I'll probably do that tomorrow evening if you are going to be in.'

'Oh, I'll be in all right' she quipped. 'I'm a reformed character. Give my regards to your mother.'

That evening I spent watching the box with my parents and turned in early. Tomorrow was going to be interesting. First with Paul and then Sleuth Truscott. It seemed strange that this police inspector wanted to interview me. After all, I hadn't even been in the country when Paul was attacked. Furthermore, I wouldn't know all Paul's acquaintances or be able to throw any light on possible motives for the assault. I would just have to wait and see. As for Paul, I would try my best to get him away from Plovermania. In that, at least, his wife was right. He could be stubborn, though, and I knew I'd have to be careful. Having been laid low as it were, it may even have strengthened his resolve to go on probing. That wouldn't be for quite a while, though.

Up in my room that night, I looked at our old school photograph taken in 1941. There we were, Paul and I. Hardly recognisable now, after more than twenty years. What a different world it was in those days! Sleepless nights in the Anderson shelter at the end of our gardens. Constant noise and a lot of fear. That terrible morning at assembly when the head announced the news of the Lindsay family.

I put the light out and fell into an uneasy sleep.

12

When I stood at Paul's bedside the following morning I could see clearly he'd had a bad time. I hoped I didn't betray my feelings by any facial expressions.

'Hello, Paul. How are they treating you?'

I asked this as lightly as I could. His head was heavily bandaged but he managed a smile.

'One or two female dragons about the place but the grub's not bad. Good of you to take leave. Heather told me about it yesterday. What's the latest from Germany?'

'We've more or less wrapped it up,' I replied. 'Looks as if the old vicar could get two visitors when the time comes.'

I went on to tell Paul about Hugo Bennecker and he pulled a face.

'Well, blow me!' he muttered. 'If Bennecker's visit doesn't lure some of the lice out of the woodwork, I don't know what will!'

'Better all round if they don't know who he is,' I said. 'There's been enough trouble without him adding to it. It ought to be a very private call, this, with as few folk knowing about it as possible. Don't you think?'

'Yes of course. I'm not likely to announce it in the *Tallingwood Times*, Mike. I'm not that thick!'

I ignored the rebuke.

'How far did you get with your enquiries, Paul? Anybody from Vernon Road still around who actually saw what happened?'

'Unfortunately not. All the Vernon Road people in 1940 have either died off or sold out. The civil defence people seem to have disappeared too. As for the police, they wouldn't put me on to anyone involved in the incident, even if they knew of one!'

I thought then, it was time to start on Paul.

'A death certificate still had to be raised in the war, even for an enemy airman. Isn't there some place where copies of these are kept?'

'Oh yes, very much so. A central registry. All that says about Neumann is, death due to multiple traumatic injuries as a result of an air crash.'

'What about police incident reports?'

'Ah, good question! So many of them were raised during the war that they had to be put into archives initially and then, after some years, shoved into the shredding machine. At least, that's what I've been told.'

'You still think documents were falsified?'

'I think it's a possibility. It's the only way the whole thing could have been hushed up. You knew my dad while he was alive?'

'Yes, of course' I replied. 'An honest solicitor and much respected by all who knew him.'

'Would you say Dad was the over-imaginative type? The sort to indulge in fantasies and the spreading of rumours?'

'No, I wouldn't. What he told your mother was intended for her ears only. Having said that, though, I assume he was passing on something to her that he had only heard about in the LDV and that's all. Nothing that he actually saw?'

'No, he didn't see it.'

Paul was frowning.

'It was never mentioned at home again either. Funny, that. Maybe it was just as well!'

I thought it was time to change tack.

'You haven't told me about the punch up. If you don't want to talk about it – that's understandable.'

Paul was quite happy to give me a blow by blow account. He seemed rather pleased with himself. When I had heard Paul's account the obvious questions came to mind.

'Well, if you did as much damage to them as you say, surely they would seek some medical attention?'

Paul blinked.

'Very likely. I told the police about that. Even had a detective inspector over from Croydon here. Rather a sinister character. He came to see me in Tallingwood before all this and tried to get me to stop digging up the past.'

111

I didn't want to disturb Paul too much but felt he should know about Truscott's call and the appointment I was to keep.

'Was this chap an Inspector Truscott by any chance?'

Paul nodded.

'The very same. Been on to you too, has he? Heather said the police were interested in you. Sorry about that, Mike. You shouldn't be involved in any of this.'

I shrugged that off.

'Nothing on my conscience. I suppose he will ask a lot of questions about you, Paul. Might be like a positive vetting interview.'

Paul smiled at this.

'He thinks I've been having an illicit affair with some married woman and fell foul of her jealous husband.'

'Well, we both know that's not true. I can pour cold water on that idea. Heather did mention this to me. Anyway, if the questioning gets a little too personal, I'll side- step it.'

At this point a young nurse appeared and told Paul it was time for his treatment.

'Oh Lord, not again.' Paul groaned.

I rose to leave.

'I'll call in again later in the week. Give you the low down on sinister Fuzz Truscott.'

'Yes, do that' said Paul. 'Thanks for coming. Take it easy, Birdman!'

We chuckled, shook hands and off I went.

It was a pleasant enough day so I decided to walk to the centre of Croydon. A lot of rebuilding had taken place in recent years. Much had to be done to repair the damage sustained in the summer of 1944. At the town hall they had erected a fine memorial to the many civilians who had perished in the flying bomb onslaught. I stood looking at that for a while and then took the broad avenue towards the police station. When I arrived, I checked in with the desk sergeant as instructed and was asked to wait. I sat for about ten minutes before a middle-aged, grey-haired man suddenly appeared at the desk. After a few words with the sergeant, he turned to me.

'Mr Kendrick? I'm Truscott. How do you do? Please come into my office. Care for a cup of divisional coffee?'

He asked that with a smile but I declined the offer and we walked down a long corridor. Truscott's office was small but tidy. We both sat on either side of the desk.

'Good of you to call in,' he began. 'Always an unpopular question this but, how long have you got?'

'Just a few days, I'm afraid.'

'How did you find Mr Channing today? I've got to see him again this week.'

'I didn't think he looked at all well. Not surprising really but he seemed alert enough.'

'How long have you known him, Mr Kendrick?'

'Since our school days during the war. You could say we grew up together.'

'Yes. Would you say he had any weaknesses?'

'No more than the rest of us. I've always regarded him as a perfectly rational man.'

'Did he ever confide to you about serious disputes with other people?'

'No. Not that I think he would do that even if he had.'

'What about drinking habits?'

'I think he may have had a problem some years ago. His job in London was a high stress one. When he gave it all up the drink problem went with it.'

'Would you say he had a happy marriage?'

'Oh, about average. Two children and an attractive wife.'

'No signs of any dalliance with other women, then?'

'Not to my knowledge. I have spent some years away in the service, though. If he ever did indulge in that sort of thing, I wouldn't know about it.'

'I see. Thank you. How long have you been in Germany on this current tour?'

'Coming up to two years now. I'm due for a posting next summer.'

'Made a lot of friends have you, German friends?'

'No. Not a lot. Just a couple. The husband is a pilot in the West German Air Force.'

'Ah yes. A professional link, then. Mrs Channing mentioned that you were doing some research in Germany on her husband's behalf.'

'That's not quite true. The vicar of our church in Tallingwood asked me to do that.'

'May I ask you what that was?'

'There's a Luftwaffe war grave in the churchyard. The vicar

thought it was odd that nobody from Germany had ever visited the plot. He wanted to try and find some relatives.'

'Any luck with that?'

'Yes. It took a long time but we managed to find somebody.'

'When you say "we", Mr Kendrick, you had some help with this?'

'That's right. My West German friend did most of the work.'

'That was good of him. No grudges against the RAF, then?'

'No. None at all. He's a keen student of military history and I think he enjoyed doing it.'

'How about you?'

'I wasn't at all keen, to be honest with you. Not at first, anyway. Padre Latimer can be very persuasive, however. He thought it was about time we really buried the hatchet.'

'Yes. I suppose if relatives were to be found they would want to know the circumstances of the crash. That would be natural enough. Mr Channing was making a lot of enquiries about that in Tallingwood. You would have known about that, of course?'

'He mentioned it, yes.'

'Did he ever tell you he thought that German pilot baled out?'

'He said there was a possibility of it and then mentioned a rumour at the time.'

'What rumour was that, Mr Kendrick?'

'The one about Plover's Green but I discounted it. You would have heard about that?'

'Yes. Not a very pleasant story. The sort of tale to keep out of the newspapers.'

'I don't think Paul Channing would dream of printing anything like that. Do you?'

'There may be some people who might. I have to keep an open mind. Did you know the RAF did a series of surveys immediately after the war – in Germany?'

'I was still at school then but I heard about the strategic bombing survey. Trying to assess the effectiveness of the bomber offensive. I think it was political. Bomber Harris, the C in C of the Command had rubbed up a lot of people the wrong way during his time.'

'The survey I have in mind was the one used in the war

crimes trials. A spin-off from Nuremberg. Ever hear about it?'

'No. Not really. I heard about the great escape from Stalag Luft 3 and the murder of fifty RAF men by the SS.'

'Yes, that was the famous one. There were others. It was a long, grisly job. It meant exhuming the bodies of quite a number of Allied aircrew. An alarming number had bullet holes in the skull. We were able to bring a few of their murderers to justice but by no means all. I wonder what Mr Channing would think about that?'

'You seem to know a great deal about the war, Inspector. Were you in the RAF?'

'The police force was a reserved occupation throughout the war. The only way you could get out of it was by volunteering for aircrew. My eyesight wasn't good enough but two friends of mine went into the RAF. Ended up on Lancasters. One got it over Karlsruhe and the other at Nuremberg. Good blokes, both of them.'

'I'm sorry to hear that, Inspector. I'm beginning to understand how you feel.'

Truscott's phone rang then and after a brief exchange he paused.

'Forgive me, Mr Kendrick, but something urgent has cropped up. I'm much obliged to you for sparing me your time. Thank you for your help.'

I stood up and we shoook hands. Truscott escorted me down a long corridor and out of the building. I watched him make for a patrol car at the drive-in and with a uniformed officer behind the wheel they sped off.

That evening I sat chatting to Heather again. I wanted to know a little more about the interviews she had over the past few weeks with the police. We discussed Paul, of course, but I didn't tell her how poorly I thought he looked.

'Who has been conducting enquiries here in Tallingwood, Heather?'

'Oh, a young chap. Name of Barber. He's been here three times now. His boss, the inspector from Croydon has only called once.'

'I don't suppose this Barber has given you any idea of how close they are to making any arrests?'

'No. None at all. I don't suppose they would, either. Did you manage to get Paul away from the war?'

'A little, yes. He seems resigned to never getting to the bottom of it all.'

'Thank God for that. I don't think I can take much more of it, Mike!'

'Is there anything you want doing this week? I'll be visiting Paul again later.'

'No thanks. Everything's fine. What are your plans tomorrow?'

'I thought I'd pop in to see this Barber at Tallingwood Station. He might have something by now. Worth a try anyway.'

'Thanks, Mike. Don't expect to get too much out of him. He just writes down everything you say. You know what they are like.'

I said I did and we spent the rest of the evening chatting about other more mundane issues. Heather seemed more relaxed when I left and I promised to keep in touch.

My week's leave was going rapidly. I didn't want to waste it.

The following morning I rang the police at Tallingwood. DC Barber agreed to see me at 10am and on arrival I was ushered into one of the interview rooms. Barber sat opposite me with his notepad out. I told him of my visit to Croydon the day before – which he knew about.

'Yes, Inspector Truscott told me about that, sir.'

'From what Mr Channing told me, I was wondering if you had any suspects lined up? If he cracked a rib or two and loosened a few teeth of his assailants, would they not seek medical treatment?'

'Not in our manor they didn't. We've checked with doctors and dentists already. If they did get treatment they wouldn't be daft enough to seek it locally. What's more, the sort of injuries they may have had could so easily have been sustained on the sports field. That's what they would tell the medical authorities.'

'Yes, I suppose they would. Mrs Channing was a bit upset at the suggestion of her husband's possible infidelity. I believe both you and Inspector Truscott broached the subject.'

'Yes, sir, we have to examine every possibility, no matter how unpleasant.'

'Your inspector seems to think that Channing's enquiries about the German war grave has a bearing on all this. Do you share his views?'

'There are a lot of people here who think Channing could have spent his time more profitably. It's almost as if he was taking the German side. What he did has caused resentment. When that sort of thing happens, the suspect list gets longer and doesn't make my job any easier.'

'These thugs that attacked Channing were young. They wouldn't remember anything about the Blitz in '40. Somebody older could have put them up to it.'

'Even harder to prove, sir. The only way we could do that is to find the culprits and get a confession out of them.'

I thanked Barber for his time and realised nothing further would come of it. As I got up to leave, he produced a slip of paper from under a file.

'We've got an old boy, a police pensioner who comes up here two mornings a week to do a spot of cleaning. He was here during the whole of the war and might be worth chatting to. He only started the part-time cleaning job last week – comes again tomorrow.'

I thought about this and decided to have a word with him. The pensioner's name was Clayton. I arranged to call in at the station during the tea break at 11 am the following day and Barber said he would fix it.

When I got home I put a call through to an old friend of mine at the Air Ministry, as it then still was. He was in Personnel, Air Secretary's branch and I suggested a lunch in London later in the week. He suggested Thursday and I agreed. I wanted to sound him out on likely postings next year. 'Nothing ventured,' I thought.

At 11 am the following morning I duly turned up at Tall-ingwood Station again. Barber was there to meet me and standing beside him was a white-haired man clad in blue dungarees. This was George Clayton, the pensioner. Barber led us into the interview room and, after making introductions, produced some coffee. I explained who I was and asked Clayton outright if he had any recollections of a German plane crashing in Vernon Road in 1940. Barber sat back and just listened – minus his notepad.

Clayton scratched his head.

'Well, it's a long time ago. We had quite a few crash sites to see in those days – most of them "ours", I'm sorry to say. The

Vernon Road one was early evening, I think. Lucky for the residents, the main area of damage was to the rear of the houses. Ruined at least three nice long gardens and burnt down a lot of trees. Some petrol was splashed over the roof tops, though, and the AFS had to be pretty nippy in putting small fires out. We couldn't get anywhere near the main site of the crash for some time. Too much heat from the fires. We see a lot of unpleasant things in police work but you get hardened to it after a while.'

I thought about this and wondered how best to jog Clayton's memory, without giving offence.

'Yes, Mr Clayton. It must have been pretty grim. An absolute miracle that no civilians up there were killed!'

'Yes, a lot of other Tallingwood civilians were not so lucky in the weeks that followed. It's hard to remember now but there were bits of engines and aircraft parts littered all over the place. Some were found at the bottom of the road – several hundred yards away from where the plane actually crashed. We had a hell of a job extricating what was left of one of the crew from a tree. The firemen and ambulance lads took quite a time getting him down as I recall. Odd that he should have been thrown clear like that during the crash. The quirks of blast, I suppose.'

Clayton was being very helpful and I knew there was a need to be tactful with him.

'They buried what you found in that tree at St Michael's churchyard, Mr Clayton. There's a name on the grave which points to a clear identification at the time. There were two men in that plane and from what you say only one body was ever recovered from it. Can you remember anything about the removal of identity discs?'

'Yes I can. They had to remove his helmet and goggles to get at them and when I took a look I remembered the name. It was Newman, I think, or the German equivalent of it.'

'Thank you, Mr Clayton. Did you ever hear about a parachute landing at Plover's Green on the same day? I'm thinking about the second member of that crew who was never accounted for.'

Clayton looked at me rather sharply and exchanged glances with Barber before answering.

'No I didn't, not officially anyway. Plover's is really out of our manor so we wouldn't have been involved in it. That comes under Coulsdon so their officers would have attended to that. I know what you're getting at though. There were rumours running around the division about a parachute landing there, but we were all far too busy in those days to dwell on such things – believe me!'

I thanked George Clayton and DC Barber for all their help and walking away from the police station I wondered whether it was worth calling in at Coulsdon. Thinking over Clayton's account of events it was clear enough what happened to Kurt Neumann. There still remained that doubt concerning Baumbach, the gunner. Something happened at Plover's Green all right and there must have been people in the Home or Foreign Office who didn't want us probing into it. In view of NATO politics and the delicacies of Anglo-German relations at the time, they could have been right. Nevertheless, the assault on Paul Channing was wrong and probably found its origin in the mind of someone in Tallingwood. I certainly wanted to find out who that was and why they had done it.

'*Vengeance is mine, saith the Lord.*'

I thought about that as I drove back home that day. What would Dieter and Lotte think about all this? Should I salve my own conscience and tell them the truth? In the end I decided not to. As Lotte would have said, 'No useful purpose would be served by it.' Not after all these years.

13

I went to see Paul again that evening and told him about my interviews with Truscott and Barber. When I related the facts about the war crimes trials, Paul sighed.

'It doesn't need a lot of imagination to work out why Truscott mentioned that. More of the same stuff. Look what they did to our airmen and probably in dozens!'

'Well, it's true isn't it? You suspect there may have been one case like it here in England. Surprising there were not more really.'

'You want me to forget about it, don't you, Mike?'

'I think it would be better all round if you did. It's caused so much trouble and resentment in Tallingwood already. Try and put it out of your mind, Paul. Heather wants that more than anything.'

'When do you think the Germans will come over?' Paul asked that with an odd expression on his face.

'That's something I shall have to find out when I get back to Rheindahlen. If they particularly want to visit Tallingwood, they had better do it before the grave is moved in the summer.'

We finished our chat with Paul telling me about his life in the ward and his occasional clashes with the nurses. I took my leave of him then and said I would call again on the Friday.

On the following day I went up to Adastral House to see my old friend, Doug Rutherford. We had served in the same squadron together some years back and had managed to keep in touch. Doug was a Cranwell graduate and obviously destined for the top one day. He was good enough to run through all the likely postings I could expect when my present ground-tour was over. It was a pretty daunting list – the usual catalogue of sheer boredom waiting there on the career horizon. None of them particularly appealed to me and I said so. We had a pub lunch and when we parted he smiled.

'Try and put a little more into this tour, Mike. If you don't, you'll end up a career flight lieutenant. Nobody of our age enjoys org and admin but it's got to be done.'

I got the message all right. It was quite clear and I wondered what sort of a mess my annual confidential reports must have been in.

My leave was nearly over and I didn't feel I had achieved very much. When I called in at the hospital to see Paul on my last day he looked brighter.

'They're going to send me home next week if I'm a good boy.'

'At least you won't have to put up with bossy nurses any more!'

'No. I shall have Heather to contend with instead. I can't see her in the role of Florence Nightingale. The sooner I get back to work the better. Lord knows what the old bat Watkins has been up to since I was put in here.'

'You always said she was efficient, Paul. Would you prefer it if she wasn't?'

'Oh, blow Watkins! It's Heather I'm worried about. We've drifted apart in so many ways, over the past two years. Almost as if we've become totally different people. I suppose all marriages end up like that. She's so easily bored.'

When I heard that, I wondered how much of an effort Heather had really made to make things up to Paul – as she said she would.

'I think you'll find things at home will be better after all this. Just take it easy and don't reproach Heather too much.'

'How come you never married, Mike? You've had plenty of girl friends in your time?'

'Depends on what you mean by "had"'.

Paul grinned.

'Some of your old flames "kissed and told", you know. At least we know you're normal!'

'Really! I won't ask you who they were. Marriage is a very demanding commitment and some men take longer to get round to it than others. If I felt I knew where I was going. What the future holds. Perhaps I'm immature, or something.'

'I don't think you take kindly to responsibility, Mike. What you need is some woman who can relieve you of that. Find a rich widow with a pub!'

'You're obviously feeling better! I've got to fly back tomorrow. Is there anything I can do before I leave?'

'Not really. From what I've heard you've done quite a lot. My spy network in Tallingwood keeps me informed, you know. I'd still like to hear when the Germans are coming. That sister and Bennecker intrigue me.'

I promised Paul I'd let him know, wished him a speedy recovery and left the ward.

The next evening I was back in Germany. On the Monday when I got to the office in Rheindahlen, George Bradley and Freddie Flynn were laughing.

'Hey mate,' said George. 'Heard the good news?'

I thought for a second.

'What's that? SASO had a cardiac arrest?'

Freddie shook his head.

'Better than that, old dear. Aitken's posted! Goes in a month's time.'

'Gentlemen' I said, 'the drinks are on me at lunch time. We won't get much work done this afternoon. I could get plastered!'

Just as I said that my phone rang. It was Dieter.

'Hello Michael. Good leave?'

I said it was.

'Look, I've been on to Düsseldorf, to Kleinerts, and had a word with Frau Kietzmann – you remember her – Old Fiddle?'

I said I did.

'Well, I was trying to get in touch with Inge Weber of course but was told her sister, the nun, died while you were on leave in England. She'd stayed on for the funeral in Bavaria and doesn't get back until this evening. We ought to allow a decent period of mourning before expecting her to resume any social engagements.'

I thanked Dieter and then told him the good news.

'I've got a lot of work to catch up on anyway. Fancy a jug or two lunch time in the mess? We're celebrating the departure of Caliban Aitken. He goes in a month's time.'

Dieter chuckled.

'OK, Michael. See you at one. You must tell me about your leave.'

Lunch time came and we gathered at the bar. Dieter was

asking me about Paul Channing and I told him what I could.

'I had a word with the vicar by the way. Told him about Bennecker and he said he'd be pleased to welcome him as well as Inge Weber. We ought to try and find out when they are likely to visit the church, Dieter.'

'Yes, of course. That's one of the things we should discuss with Frau Weber – when we get the chance. Did you say you were going up to London on your leave to find out about postings next year?'

'That's right. Had a chat with an old chum of mine in Personnel. The only slot worth considering was a Canberra conversion at Bassingbourne. At least I'd have my own command for a tour. The trouble there is, Canberras are a breeding ground for the V-force and I don't fancy ending up as a co-pilot in that outfit!'

Dieter wanted to know why not.

'They're a pretty humourless lot. Seldom any laughter in the mess. Everything done by the book. I suppose it's the constant awareness of what they are carrying around with them that makes for that. The senior commanders are a hard-nosed crowd too. They operate on the "Curtis Le May" principle.'

Dieter wanted to know what that was.

'Don't come to me with your troubles, sonny! All I want is results!' I replied.

Dieter was amused.

'What do you expect, Michael? Tea and sympathy? They're just preparing crews for a possible war with the Soviets. How else could they pave the way for that – psychologically?'

'Hopefully, with at least one smile per month! Anyway, the other alternative was the Transport Force. That would mean straight into the right-hand seat for beginners. Perhaps after five years I might clock up enough time down the routes to try my luck in civil aviation. They don't want service pilots now anyway, particularly jet-jockeys weaned on flying aircraft to their limits. Bad for the fare-paying passengers!'

Dieter then asked what else I was offered.

'Shackletons with the "kipper-fleet" for Heaven's sake! Slow death at thirty degrees west, putting up with stroppy fish-heads!'

123

Dieter grinned.

'You shouldn't be so rude to your senior service, Michael. Have you no sense of tradition?'

I said I had but not necessarily the Navy's version of it. At this point George and Freddie butted in with raised glasses.

'Here's to old Aitken,' said George. 'May Rheindahlen's loss be the Air Ministry's gain! I know Adastral's got a lot to answer for but, blimey – do they deserve that old sod?'

We downed our beers and ordered another round. Freddie thought it was time SASO was on the move and hoped we would hear something soon. George observed ruefully that one senior air staff officer was likely to be as big a pain as another, and started to sing softly:

'Stand by your beds! – here comes the Air Vice Marshal, he's got bags of Rings but he's only one arse hole!'

The mess president walked into the bar then and gave us all a dirty look. Dieter thought we should go into lunch before we ended up under close arrest. This we did and the afternoon back at the office drifted by in a haze.

During the weeks that followed I received a letter from Paul. He was at home again and expected to be allowed back to work by the end of the month. I felt relieved on reading his letter. He made no mention of the war grave or any resumption of his previous enquiries.

Dieter rang one afternoon to say he had managed to contact Inge Weber. She had accepted the Ewalts' invitation to dinner the following Saturday. I was included and Dieter wanted to know if I could make it.

'Yes. Thanks very much. I'll look forward to it. How was Frau Weber?'

'She sounded OK. What ever happened down in Passau is over now, I think. She seemed pleased to hear we had invited you too, Michael! Lotte says you better watch it!'

'Oh, come off it Dieter. Lotte's an incurable romantic! As for you – you're never happy unless indulging in erotic fantasies!'

Dieter roared with laughter.

'I consider that a compliment! Seen anything of the lovely Margaret lately?'

I said I hadn't.

'Ah!' said Dieter, 'she's been lured into a love-nest at

Laarbruch, if you ask me. Serve you right!'

I thanked Dieter for his call and said I'd bring a bottle on Saturday.

And so it was that a closer relationship with Inge Weber began for me. Looking back now over the years, I can honestly say I had never met anyone quite like her before. Quite apart from her looks, she was highly intelligent, sophisticated, witty and charming.

Lotte's dinner party was a great success. Heidi and Helga, the Ewalt daughters came down to say good night and sang a duet for the honoured guest, Inge. She was captivated. Over coffee, Dieter mentioned his posting in the spring and Lotte said how much she would miss Rheindahlen.

'We've been so lucky here,' she said. 'I doubt we shall be as happy at Oldenburg. When you've made as many good friends as we have here, it's expecting a great deal of a conventional Bundes Luftwaffe base!'

Inge nodded.

'Yes, I know how you feel. On the plus side, both you and your husband are good mixers. You will make friends anywhere.'

Lotte gave Inge one of her dazzling Dietrich smiles at this. Inge then turned to me.

'How are things in England, Mr Kendrick? Have they recovered from the Profumo scandal yet?'

I thought carefully before answering.

'It was encouraging that we had a security breach based on normal physical attractions. So many of late seem to be based on the other sort!'

Inge and the Ewalts were amused by this.

'Yes,' said Inge, 'at least that was a step in the right direction. No, I mustn't tease you, Mr Kendrick. Forgive me.'

Dieter decided to chime in at this point.

'Any decisions yet, Michael, about the future? Next summer will be here before you know it.'

I said the Canberra tour was the most appealing. Despite the V-force implications I would probably opt for this. Inge wanted to know what Canberras were. She had heard about the nuclear V-force. Dieter and Lotte lapsed into German for a quick explanation.

'A lot of responsibility,' said Inge in English, turning to me

125

again. There was a certain look in those lynx-like eyes, I seem to recall.

'Well, Frau Weber' I replied, 'there's a good deal of responsibility in all flying operations. This will be slightly different, that's all.'

Inge smiled at this.

'Yes, I'm sure it will be. By the way, can we do a deal?'

I looked a bit perplexed at this and she went on.

'If I promise not to call you Mr Kendrick, will you promise not to call me Frau Weber?'

Dieter and Lotte exchanged knowing glances and that's how it was that evening. Getting on first-name terms with a German was – well, how shall I put it, a major step forward? Towards the end of the evening, Inge made a point of saying how much she had enjoyed her visit. She turned to Lotte.

'I'd like you all to come over to dinner in Düsseldorf soon – if you can fit it in.'

Lotte said she would make a point of it. I thought Inge seemed a little hesitant and then she turned to me.

'Do you enjoy music, Michael? The London Symphony Orchestra is coming over to Düsseldorf next week. It's a good programme. I've been given a couple of tickets. Would you be interested?'

Dieter pretended to look at the ceiling and Lotte examined her finger nails.

'I should be honoured' I replied. 'What evening would that be? I could book a table at Karminski's after the concert.'

Inge said it was on Friday next at 8pm and asked me if I had her phone number. I had it all right. That was how we made our first date.

When Inge had left, the Ewalts started. Dieter flopped down on the settee and roared with laughter. Lotte went off to the kitchen to put some more coffee on.

'What's tickling you, Ewalt?' I asked.

'You British, my dear old Michael! You never cease to amaze me.'

I had a faint idea what Dieter was referring to but still wanted him to elaborate.

'What the hell are you on about?'

'You will find out on Friday, dear Michael. I promise you. Enjoy your concert and enjoy Inge Weber, too!'

If Lotte had not brought the coffee in at that moment, I would have said something rude to Dieter.

'I thought she was a dear,' said Lotte. 'She's a little older than us but not too much. I liked that dress of hers. Must have cost the earth. I hadn't got the nerve to ask her but I bet she bought it in Paris.'

Dieter eyed Lotte with amusement.

'Yes, it was obviously worn for Michael's benefit. Do you think he noticed – being British?'

Lotte feigned mock severity.

'Oh! Shut up you! Of course he noticed, didn't you, Michael?'

I took a sip of coffee before answering.

'You two are an absolute riot. A riot of romance, intrigue and innuendo. Of course I noticed. I'd have to be half blind not to!'

Lotte poured herself some coffee and continued.

'No mention of the war all evening. I liked her for that. If she ever does visit her brother's grave I wonder when she will do it?'

'I hope to broach the subject with her on Friday next,' I said. 'Our vicar is pleased about the prospect. Frau Weber may have to contact Hugo Bennecker before she goes.'

Lotte frowned.

'Frau Weber? Michael, surely it's Inge now.'

I took Lotte's hand in mine.

'You, Lotte Ewalt, are wicked! Stop teasing me!'

Dieter roared with laughter again.

'Oh, Michael! Watch out for these widows. The German species are particularly dangerous!'

'Is that so?' I retorted. 'My chum Paul Channing says I should find a rich widow with a pub! Perhaps a travel agency is the next best thing!'

'You could do a lot worse, Michael' said Lotte. 'Now that lovely Margaret has forsaken you. I had such high hopes for you there.'

Dieter still had some brandy to finish off.

'Ja! That was so sad. Just think of all those nights of unbridled passion you have missed.'

Lotte giggled and I stood up.

'I think it's about time you put your husband to bed, Lotte.

I'll keep you posted how things go on Friday. Thanks for a super evening.'

I kissed Lotte on the nose and told Dieter to finish his Asbach. They both saw me to the door and I walked back to the mess. Those were the truly happy days. I wasn't to know just how short-lived they would be.

I rang Inge the next day to tell her I had booked a table at Karminski's on Friday and she sounded pleased.

'You can leave your car outside my place, Michael. We can walk to the concert hall in ten minutes. Do us good!'

It was all fixed and the Concert was extremely good. The programme as I recall included Dvorak, Brahms, Sibelius and Elgar. It was the latter composer's *Enigma Variations* that moved the audience most. Nimrod was the one that did it. I looked around me in the concert hall that evening and saw many people in tears. If Dieter thought the British never ceased to amaze him, the Germans had the same effect on me.

Over supper at Karminski's Inge said she had heard from Hugo Bennecker.

'He's coming up to Düsseldorf at the end of the month. A business trip, I think. He was asking after you, by the way. Wanted to know when I might be able to make the trip to England. I've invited him to dinner at my place so we can discuss things. Do you have your pastor's name and address, Michael?'

I jotted it down on a piece of paper for her.

'Just let him know when you've planned your visit. He's the helpful sort and will give you all the travel info. you will need. Be prepared for tea and biscuits in the vicarage, though! He likes to natter a lot, especially about theology.'

Inge wore a faint smile at this.

'Yes, I expect he does. He's obviously tried you out. Did he have any luck?'

'Not a lot.'

'You're one of his parishioners, aren't you?'

'Not a very devout one, I'm afraid. Too many diversions. Religion and the military life don't go together. "Thou shalt not kill and beat your swords into ploughshares" might have something to do with it. The only thing Our Lord ever said to the "soldiers" was – "Offer violence to no man and be content with your wages." Not exactly an encouraging comment to the profession, was it?'

Inge gave a little laugh.

'Shame on you, Michael Kendrick! That was a very cynical observation. Better not let your pastor hear you say things like that.'

'Oh, I think he knows I'm a lost cause. I don't go to his church often enough.'

'And yet he asked you to find the Neumann family. If he thought you were that far out in the spiritual wilderness, I don't think he would have bothered!'

'Are you trying to analyse me again, Inge? It must be an occupational hazard.'

'I've always had an enquiring mind with people, even as a girl. Perhaps my job has sharpened that tendency over the years. I'm sorry if you feel I'm prying.'

'Just a little, not much. Now let me do some analysis.'

'Go ahead. I reserve the right to plead the Fifth Amendment, though.'

'That's a good old Yank expression! You West Germans have become very Americanized, haven't you. How long were you in the States?'

'Two years. It was hard work and I wasn't all that happy for the first year. Then I made some good friends and it was a lot better.'

'Any deep and profound memories or is that Fifth Amendment territory?'

'The first night I spent there was the hotel in Washington. I was alone in my room and switched on the TV. There was this very lovely British actress, Greer Garson, and I was fascinated by her. A true English rose. It was the film *Mrs Miniver* and I had not seen it before. You ever see it?'

I said I had.

Inge took a sip of her wine and continued.

'When the German pilot turned up in her kitchen and I watched that performance, you can imagine what I felt. How difficult things were going to be for me. I lay back on my bed and cried myself to sleep.'

I knew there was a need for care at this point and tried to say the right thing.

'It was a film made during the war, Inge. The Americans made it for us in Britain to keep us going.'

'Yes. I know that now. I was younger then and so unsure of myself.'

'OK, let's forget all that. Any "nice guys" around in those days?'

'That's the Amendment question really but, yes, there was one but he was married, like all the interesting men seem to be.'

'Well, that lets me off then, doesn't it,' I muttered.

'You have an expression in English, I think' said Inge. 'Stop fishing for compliments?'

'I didn't mean to. It was a reflex action. Nothing more or less. Sorry!'

'When we first met, Michael, you said you knew how I felt about bereavement in time of war. Are you ready to talk to me about that yet?'

'Not really. But I will tell you about it one day. There's a cocktail party in the mess next week. It's on Wednesday at 6pm. Think you could make it? Dieter and Lotte will be there.'

Inge toyed with her dessert.

'Can I ring you tomorrow?'

I said she could.

On the way back to the flat I thanked her for a most enjoyable evening and she looked at me then with a smile.

'I never know quite what to do or say with Englishmen on the first date. Whether to shake hands or not?'

I thought Inge needed some encouragement so I took her face in my hands and gave her an RAF Special right on the mouth!

'Don't forget the cocktail party on Wednesday, Inge. You could end up at the Ewalts. They've got a spare room.'

Inge was a little breathless.

'Thank you, Michael. I'll ring in the afternoon tomorrow. About 3pm. That be all right?'

I said it would be and climbed into the car and drove back to Rheindahlen. I knew what was happening well enough. I wondered if Inge did.

As it happened, Inge couldn't make the cocktail party. She had a group of French and Dutch business men to attend to, by director's orders. She sounded fed up when she rang through to tell me.

130

'Look Michael, it's Hannelore Keitzmann's birthday next Saturday. She's throwing a party at her place and I shall need a male escort. Can you come to my rescue?'

Remembering how pleasant Old Fiddle had been, I said I'd be delighted.

This was the beginning of frequent visits to Düsseldorf for me.

One evening in November, a high pressure system got its grip on the Continent and Inge and I were walking back from the theatre. We had enjoyed Bizet's *Carmen*. The radiation fog started early and by 11pm the visibility was down to a few yards.

'I better find a hotel, Inge' I said. 'I'm not driving back to Rheindahlen in this lot.'

'You won't need to do that. I'll put you up in the spare room. You wouldn't find a hotel room easily anyway.'

I thought about this, just for a second.

'What would the neighbours think, Inge?'

'Oh, they mind their own business. Very gallant of you to be so concerned for my reputation. I've got enough on them to keep them quiet, believe me.'

'You must tell me about it sometime.'

'No. I wouldn't do that. I respect their privacy too much!'

When we arrived at Inge's flat we had coffee. I was wondering what time the fog would clear in the morning.

'I shall look a mess tomorrow. No razor to lift the whiskers.'

'It's OK, Michael. I've got a little one you can use. I'll put a fresh blade in it for you. You'll find everything you need in the bathroom. So stop worrying.'

We sat chatting for a while until Inge stifled a yawn.

'You better show me to BOQ's, Inge.'

She knew what that meant.

'Bachelor Officers Quarters are not in regular use here, Michael.'

She said that rather evenly, I thought.

'I didn't mean that. Sorry. I must be tired. It's dulled my wits.'

She smiled and nodded.

'Go on. Get your beauty sleep. Help yourself to coffee in the morning.'

So I turned in. I heard Inge collecting the coffee cups and

eventually I fell asleep.

It must have been just before dawn, although the thick Rhineland fog still persisted. I was conscious of a slight draught on the left side of my face. Being a cold night I knew all the windows were shut. So I turned over to find out what had caused it.

There are still some people left in this world, albeit a minority now, who prefer to keep their private and personal lives very much to themselves. It is not my purpose in this narrative to indulge in salaciousness for its own sake. It was not like that anyway. When I am told that some reference has to be made to what occurred that cold November morning, because it is relevant, I tend to avoid the issue. Inge and I were no longer two separate young people any more. That morning we became as one. Wagner said it all in his *Tristan and Isolde*, *Prelude* and *Liebestod*. That is all I leave to the reader's imagination and I have nothing more to add. Not that I could, even if I tried.

☆   ☆   ☆

'I suppose you eat a hearty English breakfast?' asked Inge, filling the coffee pot some time later.

I stood behind her and put my arms around her waist.

'Why, do you think I need one?'

She turned her head around.

'Let's say you deserve one. I've got some bacon if you can face it?'

I said I'd settle for toast and coffee and Inge was apologetic for not having marmalade. She turned the radio on to catch the weather forecast and the announcer said something about the fog but it was too rapid for me.

'What time do they expect it to lift?' I asked.

'Not before midday and then it's coming down again tonight. You better make a quick getaway when it does lift or you'll be here for the rest of the week!'

'Groupie would love that' I said. 'Kendrick AWOL in Düsseldorf!'

'What's he like, your group captain? Strict, severe with a clipped moustache?'

'Oh, he's all right. Ex wartime ace. Lots of medals. A bit

intolerant of the post-war generation. Because we never went through what he did, I suppose that's understandable.'

'Yes, we are beginning to see that here in Germany. The young ones avoid the war generation like the plague.'

'Lotte Ewalt does that but Dieter doesn't. What do you make of them by the way?'

'I like them very much. Dieter has an over-developed sense of humour at times. Not very German. I suppose that's due to his job. Lotte is "all woman" and very bright. She can give another woman the once over and still be nice about it. As for little Heidi and Helga, they could charm the birds off the trees. They've inherited their mother's good looks and been spared their father's wide grin.'

'You really have put them under a microscope, haven't you!'

'You asked me what I made of them. They all seem very fond of you, Michael.'

'It's mutual. I'm going to miss them when they go. Dieter's off on a flying refresher course next month. With his experience it should only take about six weeks.'

'That's the trouble with your life. So much turbulence. Always on the move. New places and new faces. Do you ever get fed up with that?'

'I'm used to it by now. I'd probably get fidgety stuck in one slot for years on end. At least a posting every two and a half years solves the problem of working under some old rat-bag.'

Inge laughed at this. She hadn't heard that expression before.

'What about home for you, Michael. Tell me about this Tallingwood. What's it like?'

'It's a typical Surrey suburb. A nice enough place with lots of neat middle class houses and pretty gardens. You'll like the church. It's surrounded by trees and they grow flowers in abundance. It wasn't always like that, though. It was too close to Croydon and Kenley airfields for comfort during the war.'

Inge put her head to one side and was about to say something but then changed her mind.

'Go on,' I said. 'A penny for your thoughts.'

She took a deep breath before answering.

'Was it as bad as Hamburg and Dresden, Michael?'

'No, of course not. In 1940 the Luftwaffe didn't have that

capability. We still lost a lot of people despite that, particularly four years later. The VI attacks were bad.'

Inge nodded.

'Was that when you had your bereavement, Michael?'

'No, that was early on. About the same time you lost your brother. There were these three other brothers, Timothy, Mark and John. They were super kids. So full of life and laughter. I was a constant visitor to their home just before the war. Their mother was a very dear person too. Being neighbours, the brothers and I walked to school every day. When the war came, the father joined up and Mrs Lindsay was left to rear her sons alone. That is, until the autumn of 1940.'

I paused for a moment and helped myself to some coffee. Inge put her hand across the table and laid it upon mine.

'I can see you feel deeply about this. What happened?'

'Their house had no shelter in the garden. They had plenty of offers from kind neighbours, including us. Mrs Lindsay wouldn't hear of it. She had her own reasons for this I suppose, no matter how misguided. It was a form of stubborness and defiance, I suppose. It was a mistake that cost all of them their lives. The house took a direct hit. They said that even the tough firemen and civil defence crews wept when they found them. They weren't the only ones. I did my share of weeping at the funeral. I was still a kid then but old enough to feel the first rage of hate in my young life. I grew out of that in later years of course. There now, I've told you. The Lindsays were buried at our church, Inge. Their grave is not far from your brother's. I used to lay flowers on it when I was young. Others do that now.'

Inge stood up and went to the window.

'I think the fog is thinning out at last, Michael. Thank you for telling me what you did. I'm going to be away for a few weeks starting next month. Paris, Amsterdam and New York. Don't talk to any widows while I'm away!'

I promised I wouldn't.

'Give my regards to Hugo Bennecker when he calls. I owe him an invite too. Must fix something up. Dieter's farewell party would be a good time for that. Will I see you before your trip?'

'I'll certainly ring and let you know. I ought to return the Ewalts' hospitality before Dieter starts his course. We could have a quiet dinner here one evening.'

'Fog permitting,' I said. 'I better be going, Inge. It's clearing up out there now.'

She nodded, gave me a kiss and told me to drive carefully.

The drive back was patchy. Some of the fog still hung around. I was back in the mess just after lunch had been cleared away. I wasn't hungry anyway. There was one letter for me in the mail rack. It was from my parents and all seemed well at home. Mother's parting shot was she hoped I was behaving myself. As the saying goes, If our mothers only knew!'

14

When I arrived at the office next morning, Freddie Flynn told me the group captain wanted a word as soon as I got in. I stood in his office within minutes.

'Sir, you wanted me, I believe?'

'Yes, will you go over to the provost and security block at ten this morning. Group Captain Stapleton wants a chat. Don't discuss this with your colleagues in the outer office please. I've no idea what it's about, Kendrick. If anyone wants to know the reason for your absence, just tell them you're on an errand for me. All right?'

I felt decidedly odd on hearing this. I didn't care for the provost branch as a breed. I don't think anybody did. Groupie continued.

'When you've seen Group Captain Stapleton, I want a word with you myself. This preference for a posting to the Medium Bomber Force has certain implications. We can discuss it then.'

I made my usual respectful noises and departed. At ten that morning I sat in Stapleton's office. He offered me a cigarette and did his best to make me feel at ease. He sat back in his chair and started.

'As I expect you already know, we have contacts with the West Germans on security matters at this headquarters. We get on with them very well and try to help them whenever we can. As you have been positively vetted and know all about the Official Secrets Act, I won't insult your intelligence by reminding you of your obligations in that respect. Everything I have to say to you now, falls under that Act, Kendrick!'

I said I understood well enough.

'Good. Then I can make a modest start.'

He said this with a friendly smile. Producing a photograph of Inge Weber from a file, he passed it on to me.

'You know this lady, I believe?'

136

I said I did.

'Well, the Germans tell us that in her younger days, as an undergrad at Munich University, in common with a lot of other students in the immediate post-war period, she was profoundly disturbed by the concentration camp revelations. All this had an emotional and psychological effect on impressionable young minds. When they realised the stench and decay of fascism, there was a backlash. So much so that many began to flirt with the antithesis. In this lady's case, it was a full-blown love affair. There was no question of actually joining the Communist Party, but she did live with this young man.'

He produced another photograph of a truculent youth staring into the camera.

'This chap is one Gerhardt Richter. He's changed a lot since this was taken, as you will see later. In the early fifties Richter went East. As a dedicated communist he went to the Soviet Union to study Russian and the Germans tell us he returned to the GDR two years later. He has been working for the MFS ever since.'

I didn't know what that meant and I asked Stapleton to explain.

'Ministerium für Sicherheitsdienst – the East German counter-intelligence service. Richter has been quite active and seems good at his job. So good in fact that the West Germans have made a point of keeping close tabs on him whenever they could. The lady in this case was questioned by them when Richter departed East. She told them then, that she and Richter had started to quarrel just before they graduated. She was beginning to detect the flaws and fallacies in many of his doctrines and what was more to the point, she was getting bored with him. So Inge Neumann, as she was then, had started to grow up. The West Germans said she was very helpful and told them a lot about Richter. That was on the credit side. Last year however, and this was twelve years after Richter had flown, she went to Berlin for a trade conference. Exactly how Richter had managed to get over the Wall into West Berlin is something they're still working on. In any event he was soon spotted and tailed. It had all the appearances of a chance meeting on the Kurfüsten Damm between Richter and his old flame. They had a drink together and quite a long chat.

One theory is, that she could have done this for old time's sake. Take a look at this.'

He produced a third photograph and he was certainly right about the changes in Richter's appearance. Inge looked rather sad, I thought.

'Would you like some coffee?' asked Stapleton.

I could have used something stronger but settled for the caffeine. He pressed a buzzer and a young WRAF corporal produced the cups within seconds. I was impressed. Stapleton continued.

'Despite what the Germans have done in two world wars, there's still a very strong romantic, sentimental streak in them. Theory number one suggests this was her only motive for agreeing to that tête-à- tête with Richter. The second theory takes a less charitable view. Somehow, that chance meeting could have been a pure fake. If it was pre-arranged then we have a problem on our hands. If Richter is agent-running, then with all her connections and travels she could be of extreme importance to MFS. The boys at Bonn have made no approach to her so far. They just want to know who her friends are. I'm sorry, Kendrick, but this may be embarrassing.'

He offered me another cigarette, which I accepted.

'It's got to the point of pillow-talk for you and Inge Weber, hasn't it?'

It was pointless to deny it. Inge had more than just neighbours watching her in that block of flats.

'You seem to know the answer to that already, sir. I would like to point out, with respect, that it was we who sought her out and not the other way round. She lost a brother in the war and he's buried in my home town. I was asked to trace any relatives.'

'Yes, we know all about that. When you say "we" that means Captain Ewalt, I assume?'

I said that was correct and asked if Dieter was being similarly interviewed.

'I don't know. That would be up to the Ministry of the Interior in Bonn and the Bundes Luftwaffe. Either way, you must say nothing to Ewalt about all this. He's leaving here shortly anyway. I'm more concerned about you. If at any time this lady in Düsseldorf shows even the remotest interest in this headquarters and NATO, I want to know about it. In short, what I'm telling you to do is carry on as if this conversation never took place. As the days and, no doubt nights go by, you may be able to find out a little more for us. If she is forthcoming about her early life, so much the better. You've got about six months left to serve here I'm told. As a matter of courtesy, I shall be seeing your own group captain after this. So try not to look too surprised when I walk into his office. I think that's it. Any questions?'

I was far too stunned for that.

'OK, thank you for coming to see us.'

That smile again and the hand shake. I'll never forget that day, ever.

When I got back to the office, George Bradley looked up from his desk.

'What's up, mate? Look as if you've seen a ghost!'

I parried this with a riposte George would understand.

'Heavy night out yesterday, George. Haven't quite recovered from it yet.'

Freddie Flynn put his hands together.

'There will be a two minute silence for poor officer Kendrick!'

George was quick to respond.

'Knock it off, Freddie. Can't you see he's suffering? Plastered all over the weekend and then summoned to the presence first thing this morning. What have you been up to Mike, or is that classified?'

I didn't know whether to laugh or cry at that. Trust old George to hit the nail on the head, in this case without knowing it.

'I'll be all right when I've had a good lunch, chaps. What time is it?'

Freddie shook his head in dismay.

'It's only 11.30, Mike. Think you can hang on for another hour?'

I doubted it and said so.

'Oh dear departing soul, not long for this world' intoned Freddie.

George wasn't going to let him get away with that.

'You know what you are, Flynn? A frustrated dog- collar! What the hell are you doing in our air force anyway?'

Freddie gazed aloft.

'Up there, dear boy, there is a land of eternal sunshine, above the clouds they say but, the sky is a lonely place!'

George spluttered.

'Bloody hell, he's off his trolley, Mike. Do you think we ought to report it to Groupie?'

I had to laugh at this stage.

'OK, chaps, you've cheered me up. Mission completed. Hair of the dog in the bar at 12.30.'

We got down to our org and admin chores then. At around midday, Stapleton turned up. I pretended not to notice his arrival and he swept into our group captain's office as if he owned the place. While he was in there I kept thinking about our meeting. He could have handled things differently if he chose but he didn't. For the first time in my life, I felt a tinge of respect for his branch of the service. They had a lousy job to do, from corporal SP on the base to group captain at HQ. I felt I had been let off lightly – one way or another. Stapleton spent half an hour with Groupie and that was it. They left together just after 12.30 and my bet was they would repair to the mess for lunch. I had planned to sip a quiet beer with George and Freddie but remembered Groupie's threat to discuss the Canberra tour.

'On second thoughts, chaps, I'll just take lunch' I announced. 'My future is being decided this afternoon. Ought to keep a clear head for that.'

George grimaced and Freddie shook his head.

'Two confessionals with Groupie in one day, Mike? Hope you get absolution, mate!'

After lunch I was back in Groupie's office just after three. He was studying my annual confidential report and then looked up and spoke.

'Well now, Group Captain Stapleton has told me all I need to know about the subject of your interview this morning. You will be reporting to him in the first instance and to me thereafter. This, in the event of any developments. Now then, this preference for posting. I don't honestly think the Air Secretary's branch will wear it. As a Canberra tour invariably leads to the V-force, there are certain qualities required in that role. One of these is a total commitment to the service and I know the present C in C only wants dedicated high quality officers in his command. Do you feel that you fall into that

140

category, Kendrick?'

I said I tried to – rather lamely.

'It takes a certain temperament to succeed in the V-force and I'm not at all sure that you were born with it.'

I said I was sorry to hear that.

'I don't think you are sorry at all!' said Groupie. 'You couldn't care less, could you? Come on, be honest.'

'A Canberra tour would give me captaincy experience, sir, I care about that.'

'You could get that in other commands in due course. What exactly do you want later on? Your present engagement runs out when you reach the ripe old age of thirty-eight. Are you telling me you intend a full career beyond that age? If so, you're going to have a struggle. Competition is very fierce for permanent commissions to fifty-five. Only officers who excel in every posting they're given stand a chance. Do you think you've excelled in this posting?'

I had to agree I hadn't.

'No' said Groupie, 'you bet you haven't! Org and admin has been a pain in the butt to you and you've made little effort to disguise it! For Heaven's sake, man, brace-up and start behaving like a professional!'

There was no reply to that and Groupie continued.

'As for those other two sons of darkness out there, your immediate colleagues, I'm not sure which one of you is – Oh, never mind. You didn't hear that!'

I felt sorry for George and Freddie and wondered what their reports were going to look like. Groupie folded my report with a flourish.

'I'm going to recommend a tour with the Transport Force. It's important work and very demanding on flying skills and captaincy. Try and impart some of your previous enthusiasm for flying duties in your current appointment. That's all.'

I came out of Groupie's office with this thought in mind – 'Streuth, what a bloody awful day!'

When George Bradley told me Wing Commander Aitken wanted me I nearly collapsed on the spot.

'What the hell does he want?'

George grinned.

'His relief has arrived. Wants you to get acquainted. Try and be polite, Mike. This could be the happiest day of your life.'

Freddie suddenly chipped in.

'It's a WRAF wing commander, Mike! Aitken's livid!'

We all burst into laughter and Freddie couldn't resist the obvious comment.

'Takes one old woman to relieve another – they say!'

George was about to add something to this when my phone rang. It was Dieter.

'Michael, my course has been brought forward. I'm off in the morning. To make matters worse Inge rang to invite us all over to Düsseldorf on Saturday.'

'I'm sorry, Dieter. We shall just have to fit it in later! A bit sudden isn't it?'

'It certainly is. Major Max is fed up. My relief doesn't arrive until next month.'

'Will you get any leave during the course?'

'I don't know. I doubt it. Lotte's fuming. Had a lot of harsh things to say about NATO and the Bundes Luftwaffe. I had no idea she knew so many naughty words!'

'Well, Dieter. Not to worry. I'll pop round and see Lotte later in the week. Keep smiling. Have a good course.'

'Will you have a word with Inge, Michael? She's been trying to get through to you all day. RAF lines were busy she was told.'

I said I'd ring her that evening. With that, Dieter said he had to dash off somewhere and the call ended.

I made a brief visit to Wing Commander Aitken's office and met his relief. She was a pleasant surprise. A good strong hand shake and a sense of humour. Aitken didn't look too pleased. He probably thought she would be too easy on me in the coming months – or something.

That evening back in the mess I rang Inge but there was no reply. I thought of putting a call through to Hanne Kietzmann but decided against it. I needn't have worried. After dinner, as I sat in the ante-room, the reception desk called for me on the PA system. When I got to the phone, it was Inge.

'How are you, Michael? Had a busy day?'

'Not bad,' I lied, 'how about you?'

'Very busy indeed. I didn't get in until late. I do wish the French were as easy to do business with as the Dutch. You know about Dieter, Michael?'

'Yes. He rang this afternoon. Lotte's up in arms about it.'

'I expect she will get over it. Women do, you know. We shall just have to arrange that little dinner foursome later. Will I see you this weekend?'

'Provided nothing untoward crops up, yes. When would I be allowed over?'

'Allowed, Michael? That's a funny word to use.'

'I'm a funny bloke. Hadn't you noticed?'

'All right, funny man! Come over Friday evening if you can. Hanne's got a gentleman friend – at long last. I've invited them for drinks and a modest supper. Hanne's rather excited about it. I hope she won't get hurt. She's such a dear.'

'Well done, Hanne! I think she's far too sensible for emotional injuries of that sort.'

'Don't you believe it! She's been on her own for far too long. Out of practice with men and vulnerable.'

'Well, I reckon we could give this chap the full analysis, Inge, don't you?'

'Are you laughing at me, Michael?'

'I wouldn't dare! How old is this bod anyway? Hanne's generation I hope.'

'Yes. He's a lonely widower, she says. They can be quite devastating, you know.'

'Really! That sounds interesting. I think Friday evening has promise.'

'You wait until I see you, Michael Kendrick! Perhaps you'll be in a better mood by then. Try and make it by 8 pm please.'

I said I'd be on time and that was it.

As I walked back to my room, I wondered if that call had been monitored. Some of them were. In view of what happened earlier that day, there was more than an even chance that it had been.

The rest of the week went by and my weekend in Düsseldorf with it. Nothing of any significance came out of it.

I looked up Group Captain Stapleton in the Air Force List on the following Monday. Among his many qualifications, decorations etc., I noticed he was a barrister at law. That didn't surprise me at all.

I called in to see Lotte that evening and told her about the very pleasant and amusing supper with Inge on the previous Friday. We sat in the lounge and Lotte listened intently.

'Hannelore Kietzmann might not be the only one to get hurt, Michael.'

'What makes you say that, Lotte?'

'Don't misunderstand me, Michael dear. I like Inge Weber, but you've never met anyone quite like her before, have you?'

I had to admit that was true.

'You say Inge is an analyst – of other people. Women are pretty good at this. Have you been seeing a lot of her, Michael? I think you know what I mean by that!'

'We are good friends, Lotte. I'm just beginning to feel there may be something more to it than that.'

That was a defensive statement and Lotte knew it.

'Oh, my dear Michael, be careful! Inge is a successful business woman with a very high-powered job. The world is changing and no more so than here in Germany. What you have to decide, my dear, is this. Is Inge Weber the great love of your life or is she just a ruthless predator who takes the occasional lover when the need arises?'

I was flabbergasted at that and Lotte could see it written all over my face.

'Women see through eachother so much better, Michael. Because Dieter and I are more than just fond of you! Oh dear, I'm making such a mess of this!'

I took Lotte by the hand.

'You're not making a mess of anything. I know what you're trying to say and believe me, I appreciate it. I'm thirty-two years old, Lotte, and supposed to be a big boy now. It takes longer for some of us to mature than others you know. It's nice to know I've got dear friends like you and Dieter who care.'

Heidi and Helga suddenly appeared at the bottom of the stairs. Helga was tearful. A nightmare had awakened her so I gave her a cuddle. In my fractured German I told her I would take her one day in my 'Flugzeug' and we would soar above the clouds together, she and I. Lotte bit her lip at that and I knew it was time to go. As I stood at the door I remember saying this to Lotte.

'Cheer up, Mum. Dad Dieter will be home again before you know it. Then we shall have a party they will talk about for months!'

Lotte gathered her little ones around her and nodded.

'Remember what I said, Michael. I was serious, you know!'

I had seldom seen Lotte in such a mood. There was something more than my love life on her mind. Was it a premonition of some kind? If it was, I wasn't to know of it then.

☆ ☆ ☆

Dieter Ewalt was to spend the first two weeks of his course in the ground school. This was to catch up with the systems and learn in detail about the new equipment that had been installed. When the flying programme started he spent the first few hours putting everything he had learned into practice. Circuit work, high altitude familiarisation, high speed runs, weapons training and formation flying. In this latter aspect of the course he found some of his fellow students in more need of practice than others. Always an exacting facet of flying, Dieter would land off some of those sorties bathed in perspiration. Despite that, he was enjoying things immensely and had no regrets at saying farewell to his Flight Safety desk at Rheindahlen. What he enjoyed most was the camaraderie in the crew room and the mess. He was back again where he felt he truly belonged. There were three USAF instructors on the staff. One of them, Major Skipton, had trained Dieter in the United States some years before. They sat chatting in the crew room one day. The American was a large man with a crew cut and a bluff manner.

'You're doing OK, Dieter. You haven't lost your touch. Wish I could say the same for some of the others! That's the trouble with this racket, shove your butt into a chair for a couple of years and you come back as green as a cadet!'

He pronounced the last word at Kay-det. Large USAF Major continued.

'At least you spent your staff assignment in Flight Safety. You've obviously been following the "sharp end", as the RAF would say. How was Rheindahlen, Dieter? Rugged duty?'

'Piece of cake, old boy – to use another RAF expression. It could have been a lot worse. I was lucky in finding a good buddy in the RAF. We got on just fine!'

The USAF major produced an enormous cigar and offered Dieter one which he declined.

'Yeah, I like the limeys too. Some of the guys don't. It's that accent that bugs them, I guess, but you get used to it. When

145

you find out what really makes them tick, they're some of the best flyers in NATO . No kiddin!'

Dieter thought how proud I would have been to hear that. He promised himself to tell me about it one day. The USAF major suddenly removed his bulk from the crew room chair.

'Think you could hack a formation mission in the lead tomorrow Dieter? If you're going to be a major at the end of this junket, you better get some lead-time in!'

Dieter nodded.

'That makes good sense, thanks for the confidence.'

The American put a large paw on Dieter's shoulder.

'No sweat, kid. You've earned it – see you!'

15

At 5 pm one Tuesday afternoon I was beginning to put the final touches to another report. It would have to run the editorial gauntlet the next day and, if Groupie didn't pick holes in it, then Wing Commander Aitken certainly would. George and Freddie were collecting their papers together and asked me if I would mind locking up for them. I couldn't resist the jibe.

'Officers Bradley and Flynn displaying escapist tendencies again?'

George shrugged.

'You haven't got a wife like Freddie and I. As a carefree bachelor, you ought to be pleased to smooth the path of matrimony.'

'Go on. Buzz off, Bradley, and take the sanctimonious Flynn with you!'

Freddie looked hurt.

'You'll never get to heaven, Mike!'

George giggled and I lowered my gaze to the papers before me. Within a few minutes I was alone in the office when suddenly Groupie appeared at the door. He held his hand out and spoke to me.

'Can you spare me a minute?'

He looked very strained and I had never heard him address me in that manner before. I got up and walked into the office marked on the door with Groupie's full title, Group Captain A.R. Templewood, C.B.E., D.F.C., A.F.C. To my utter amazement he had a bottle of brandy on his desk, flanked by two glasses.

'Sit down, Mike' he said.

He had never called me by my Christian name in the two years I'd worked for him. Something was terribly amiss. Groupie and I sat facing one another and he began.

147

'During the war when things were very bad, I got to know and get fond of a lot of fine friends. We were losing so many crews in those days, Mike. You were lucky to survive a tour of Ops in Bomber Command and the average ended long before that. The shock of those losses in the early days had an unsettling effect on me. I wasn't sure I had the stamina to carry on but carry on I did. I saw so much of this in '43 and '44. In most cases, I had a grandstand view of my friend's demise which made it so much worse. In peace time, we don't have to go through that nearly so often, thank God.'

I was not in the habit of interrupting my group captain but, on this occasion, I made an exception.

'It's Dieter Ewalt, isn't it, sir?'

'Yes, Mike. I'm afraid it is. It happened this morning off Heligoland.'

At this point he poured a measure of brandy and offered it to me.

'No thank you, sir. What happened, exactly?'

Groupie looked a little relieved and the brandy remained untouched.

'I spoke to Major Litjens this afternoon. He said Ewalt was leading a section of four. They were on a formation practice sortie and, when changing over from echelon port to starboard, one of the boys slammed his wing tip into Ewalt's cockpit canopy. He wouldn't have known much about it. That's one consolation at least. Those F104s disintegrated into a lot of tiny fragments, according to others in the formation. It's still under investigation of course, but there may be some question of control or actuator failure in this case. The trouble is, as we both know, there's so little to go on. Pilot error on the part of Ewalt's wing-man will probably be the board's finding. Major Litjens and Colonel Letzlinger are handling all this and what makes it worse, they were as fond of Ewalt as you were!'

My mind was reeling at all this but I managed to collect my thoughts.

'What about Ewalt's wife? I blurted out. 'When was she informed?'

I'd forgotten to address Groupie properly but he overlooked that.

'Lunch time today,' he replied. 'She's under sedation and has two of the wives with her now. You won't be able to see her for forty-eight hours at least. Not according to the principal medical officer.'

'Thank you for telling me, sir, particularly in the way you did.'

I nearly added that I didn't think he had it in him, but didn't. They say the eyes are the mirrors of the soul and Groupie may have sensed my thoughts when he looked into mine that terrible afternoon.

'You have taken this a lot better than I thought you would, Mike. This sort of thing ever happen to you before?'

'Yes, sir. A couple of times at Leuchars, but this is the big one for me.'

'I know it is, boy. It's going to upset a lot of people here, my wife included. Before you go and see Ewalt's widow, call round and have a word with Mrs Templeton; she's been with Lotte since this happened. Always a good idea to know what you're in for. Sure you won't have that brandy now?'

I said no to that and stood up, sensing the interview was over.

'If you don't mind, sir. I'd like to collect my papers now and go back to the mess.'

'Yes, Mike. You do that. It will take a day or two before this whole tragedy sinks in. At least, that's how it was for me when I was your age. Does that surprise you?'

There was no answer to that either. I could have made some trite comment but didn't. I just stood there and shook my head.

'Good night, sir,' and I walked out of Groupie's office.

When I got back to my room, I just sat on the edge of my bed and stared at the floor. How long I stayed like that I've no idea. It must have been quite a while. At length there was a knock on my door and without looking up I called out, 'Come in.'

It was Freddie Flynn. He closed the door behind him.

'I've just heard about your chum, Mike. Are you all right?'

As Freddie sat himself down on my easy chair I turned to look at him.

'He was all that's best in Germany, Fred. To me, he was the brother I never had. He was an airman and knew what the risks were. It's his widow and little ones that grip me by the guts – and you ask me if I feel all right?'

149

'Take it easy, Mike. I was just trying to help.'

'Why you, Fred? Why did they decide to send you – because you're the religious one?'

'George can be a bit blunt at times. Perhaps they thought I would be able to find the right words. It's not good for you to be sitting here alone like this, Mike. Come back with me to my quarter. Sybil's got the spare room bridged up.'

'How did you hear about it, Fred?'

'Groupie's wife rang Sybil and then had a word with me. I think the old man's a bit worried about you. Said something about being the one to have to break the news.'

'Does he think I'm unstable or something?'

'There was no mention of that at all. Mrs Templewood knows how close you are to the Ewalts and didn't want you to be on your own tonight.'

'She can save all her sympathy, strength and support for Lotte and those kids! God knows they're going to need it.'

'Come on, Mike. Grab your small kit. We'll have a quick snort in the bar before we go!'

Down in the foyer I left my grip bag at Reception and Freddie led the way to the bar. It was rather crowded and we had to go near the end of the bar to get served. Just on our right, Wing Commander Aitken, his WRAF relief and two other officers were standing in a little group. It must have been a farewell party of some kind and Aitken looked flushed. It was rare to see him in the bar and Freddie gave me a knowing look. We couldn't help hearing snatches of their conversation. One of them mentioned a news flash on the German TV network. The mid-air collision of two F104s had been released that evening. I just couldn't believe what happened next. Aitken downed the remains of his glass and putting it on the bar, said: 'As far as I'm concerned, that's two Krauts less to worry about!'

The others in that group looked uncomfortable. Paul Channing had told me I had a short fuse once. That night the fuse was lit and it ran fizzling until it erupted into blind fury.

I turned to face Aitken and let him have it, loud and clear on all channels.

'Dieter Ewalt was worth ten of you – as an officer and a man!'

Aitken clenched his fists and glared.

'How dare you speak to me like that! I'll have you court martialled for gross insubordination!'

That did it. Although Freddie had taken hold of my left arm I broke free and within inches of that hated face, the final explosion took place.

'You go to hell – you paralytic old goat!'

Aitken stood open-mouthed and his WRAF relief went white. One of the other officers in the group, a squadron leader, stepped forward and addressed Freddie.

'Take this officer out of here and confine him to his quarters!'

'Yes, sir' said Freddie. 'May I speak to you for a moment outside?'

'No, you cannot' said the squadron leader. 'I've given you an order, now carry it out!'

'It's all right Fred,' I said, 'I'll come quietly.'

When we got into the foyer I collected my grip and Freddie was clearly shaken.

'I'll have to ring Groupie about this, Mike. I'm sorry but I was under orders to take you home with me tonight. This incident changes all that. You do see that, don't you?'

'I'm the one who should be sorry, Fred, for getting you mixed up in all this. Thank Sybil for me when you get home. I'm turning in now under my own steam. See you later.'

With that, I mounted the staircase and went slowly to my room. So ended Black Tuesday!

In the morning just after breakfast, I took a call from the reception desk. It was from Russ Tillis, PA to SASO. Russ was another up and coming squadron leader and a contemporary of Doug Rutherford's at Cranwell. Perhaps rather more conscious of his rank at an early age than Doug was, he was nevertheless approachable.

'Hello Mike, how goes it?'

'Well enough, thank you, sir, under the circumstances.'

'Yes. It's not been the best of weeks, has it. Look, I've had to make arrangements for SASO to see you today. It will mean best bib and tucker, I'm afraid. Number One Service Dress. Hope you've got a decent cap to wear?'

'I've only worn it twice since I bought it.'

'Well, that ought to do. You better get over here at five to twelve, Mike. SASO wants to see you at twelve. Don't go to your office this morning. I'll square all that with Group Captain Templewood, OK?'

It was far from OK but I knew Russ was just doing his job. 'Yes sir, five to twelve.'

No flight lieutenant in his right mind likes interviews with air vice marshals. They tend to be one- sided affairs.

I sat in the ante-room for a while imagining what High Noon was going to be like. SASO would be wearing the gun belt and I would just be standing there in No 1 SD without so much as a pea-shooter! When the appointed time approached, I stood in Russ Tillis's outer office and glanced at what was written on SASO's door. All those honours, orders and decorations. The list was daunting. Russ probably read my thoughts.

'SASO will do all the talking, Mike. Try not to say anything unless you really have to. You'd do yourself a favour if you took my advice. When it's over, I've got some things for you, by the way.'

A buzzer went on Russ's desk and it was the signal for me to pass through that awesome door. I marched in, came to a halt and saluted. SASO had a pile of papers on his desk and he was writing quickly. He didn't look up at all for at least half a minute and I stood there at attention. Finally, when he did look up, he removed his horn-rimmed spectacles and examined me from head to toe. The thought did cross my mind that he was measuring me up for a coffin! Perhaps he was, metaphorically speaking. There were two silver models on his desk. A Typhoon and a Javelin. He leaned back in his chair and in a voice so full of authority, he began.

'I want you to understand why I am sending you home tomorrow. This whole question of giving way to our feelings and losing that vital self-control destroys the very fabric of discipline, and without that no fighting service can survive. In time of war, the enemy would give us no lee-way for that. The NATO alliance has to prepare for a possible war, which is why we are all here. In a civilian environment, such things as provocation, mitigating circumstances, emotional upheavals and stress may or may not be taken into consideration in some cases. We can never do that. There are demands made on us in this profession which not all people can meet. It may be fashionable in some quarters to sneer at the military virtues. I don't regard them as virtues at all. They are essential require-

ments. You must read your commissioning scroll again sometime. When our sovereign Head of State appointed you as an
officer – the words, "We, reposing special Trust and Confidence in your Loyalty, Courage and DISCIPLINE", were
used. That word discipline appears twice in that scroll. Not just
for yourself but for others too. It raises the burning issue of
Example. Quite clearly, your conduct on Tuesday failed to
meet that. There are other reasons why I cannot retain you on
my staff. This liaison in Düsseldorf with a lady who may have
some questionable political affiliations is charged with doubts
in my mind. To assist Group Captain Stapleton would require
self- control of the highest order and this you do not appear to
possess. You will return to your quarters and pack your
personal belongings. Tomorrow at 11.00 you will be flown
from Wildenrath to Northolt. On arrival there you will report
to the adjutant of the Holding Unit at Uxbridge and await
further orders. Depending upon subsequent enquiries here, you
may be the subject of a summary of evidence. Failing that, the
Air Secretary will decide what is to be done with you. That's
all!'

I saluted, did an about-turn and left. As I entered Russ's
office he stood up.

'How was it?' he asked.

'A bit like the Last Judgement!'

'Yes. I can imagine. The old man doesn't mince his words
much, does he?'

'Everything he said was right, of course. Somewhere along
the line, I've lost my way all right. He brought that home – in
no uncertain terms.'

Russ gave a quick glance at SASO's door.

'Look Mike, I shouldn't be telling you this really but I'm
going to anyway. Your Groupie spent half an hour with SASO
this morning. I only picked up snatches of it and I can tell you
this. He fought like a lion in there for you. Later on, Wing
Commander Aitken was here. He was only in with SASO for
ten minutes but he came out looking like death warmed up!
That's just for you. Do me a favour and keep it to yourself.'

I promised I would.

'Well, here are the documents you will need. Travel author-
isation and all the rest. I'm sending a signal to Uxbridge this
afternoon with copies to Air Ministry. Good luck, Mike.'

We shook hands and as I walked back to the mess to pack my personal belongings, I thought about Russ Tillis and Doug Rutherford. If young officers like them were to be the air marshals of tomorrow, then I knew the future of my service was going to be in good hands.

Back in my room, I looked around and took my cases down from the top of the built-in wardrobe. There was another knock on my door. This time, I opened it myself and standing there was Groupie.

'Can I come in?' he asked.

'Yes, sir, of course.'

I bade him sit down and he began.

'A great deal has happened in a very short space of time and none of it good. Your colleagues Bradley and Flynn are busy at the moment doing your job as well as their own. As there isn't time for any hand-over as such, they are going to have their heads down until your relief arrives. They wanted to come over and see you this evening but I've told them not to. It just wouldn't be appropriate. You couldn't use the bar anyway. You'll see them again in Blighty soon enough!'

'Yes, sir. How is Mrs Ewalt?'

'She's coming out of shock, gradually. Colonel Letzlinger's wife and mine have been kept busy too. It's the children they are worried about. They haven't told them yet. Mrs Letzlinger is working on that.'

'Any date fixed for the funeral?'

'No. Not yet. My wife and I will go to it when the time comes.'

'Mrs Ewalt will want to know what's happened to me, sir.'

'Yes, and so will somebody else. Have you had time to make any calls to Düsseldorf?'

'No, sir. I haven't. Everything else has put that right out of my mind.'

'Well, don't worry about Mrs Ewalt. My wife will tell her about you in due course. The facts behind your departure will never be disclosed. We shall think of a suitable version. When you get to Uxbridge you'll have time to pen a letter of condolence. That's all I can suggest.'

'It just seems so inadequate, sir. What about Düsseldorf?'

'What about it?'

'I'd like to make a call. By now the names of those involved

154

in the — '

Groupie didn't let me finish.

'If you want my honest opinion and I offer it on a man to man basis, I don't think this is the right time to do that. It just so happens that your friend in Düsseldorf did read the crash report in the press. She rang the Ewalt quarter and Mrs Letzlinger answered it. That happened this morning and from what I gather, it was an emotionally charged conversation. Young Bradley took a call for you on your extension shortly afterwards. Under my instructions, he informed the caller you had returned to England unexpectedly. That incoming call Bradley took was from Düsseldorf!'

'They seem to have thought of everything. Does this mean I'm not permitted any further contact with Düsseldorf – on an official level?'

'No, it doesn't. It's just that right now, we feel it would be better if you didn't. Let the dust settle first, boy. If, in the passage of time, you wrote to your friend and resumed matters, you would still be obliged to follow Group Captain Stapleton's instructions. It would be handled by someone else in England, of course.'

'I see.'

'I hope you do. As long as the West Germans hold reservations about your friend, I see no other alternative for you.'

'Supposing they find out they're wrong, sir. Been wrong all the time. What then?'

'They would tell you about that at home, soon enough. I don't need to know this but . . . Oh never mind! It's time I was going anyway.'

Groupie stood up and made for the door.

'Looks like you've got a lot of packing to do. MT is picking you up after breakfast tomorrow to catch that Pembroke from Wildernrath. Good luck and try to stay out of trouble!'

He said that with a faint smile. We shook hands and he was gone.

I didn't sleep too well that night. Far too many loose ends left behind in Germany for my liking. Letters would never express what I felt to Lotte and Inge. Perhaps I was becoming paranoid too and this worried me. I woke up in a sweat about 3am and didn't get to sleep again either. I put in an early appearance at breakfast but wasn't hungry. As I came out of

155

the dining room, who should be standing in the ante-room but George and Freddie. They must have got up early themselves to do this. George spoke first.

'You didn't think we would let you go without wishing you all the best, did you? Groupie told us he was seeing you last night so we kept out of the way.'

I thought it was a neat way of putting it and managed a smile.

'Good of you to come. Sorry about all the extra work I've let you in for.'

'Oh, bugger the work!' snorted George. 'Let us know what happens, won't you?'

I said I would. Freddie then offered his hand.

'No matter what happens, Mike, I want you to know I've enjoyed working with you. Sybil sends her love. As George says, do keep in touch!'

It was the best farewell we could manage; the bar wasn't open either which was just as well. I looked at them and gave a parting shot.

'Keep an eye on Bradley's spiritual welfare, Fred. You know what a sacrilegious bastard he is!'

They both laughed. I spotted the Wildenrath bus outside the mess then and George and Freddie helped me with my cases to board it. As the bus pulled out, they stood and waved. Within another hour I was on my way home. I watched the landscape below and wondered when I would ever see Germany again. The two years I had spent there had passed quickly enough. 'If only things had been different,' I thought. I suddenly felt very tired. It must have been my broken night. I closed my eyes and settled back in the seat for a snooze. I fell into a deep sleep in fact and had another disturbing dream. I kept seeing Lotte and Inge at the end of a long tunnel and as I ran to them, they receded further and further away.

16

'Wake up, sir' said a sergeant, 'we're at Northolt. Are you all right?'

He looked a little anxious. I was perspiring and it didn't look right to the sergeant. It was cold in that Pembroke and even colder on the tarmac.

'I think I'm all right, thank you. Must have picked up a bug in Germany.'

The sergeant nodded.

'Customs will be here in a minute, sir' and he passed to the rear to unlock the door.

The formalities over, another mini-bus conveyed me to Uxbridge. The journey there from Northolt through central London was tedious. When we arrived at the mess, I was allocated a room and the young WRAF at reception handed me an envelope. It was from the adjutant of the Holding Unit. It said simply, 'Get some rest. When you feel up to it, come and see me tomorrow.' I noticed the author was a flight lieutenant. That would help at least.

I slept better that first night at Uxbridge. After breakfast the next day I checked in with the adjutant. He was a man in his early fifties with a kindly manner. Commissioned late in life I thought, probably an ex NCO.

'It's going to be a while I think before we know what's next. I expect you would like some leave but that's not possible at the moment. I'm sorry. There's a fair amount of paper work to be done here. Amendment lists, inventory checks and the like. I could certainly find plenty for you to do!'

'All right. If the devil finds work for idle hands I better get stuck into another dose of admin.'

'It won't be for long. Cheer up,' he said with a smile. 'It'll be better than moping around in the mess. You're not exactly confined to the station but we are near the centre of London.

Soho is a place to be avoided, they tell me!'

'Thanks for the advice. I have heard of Raymond's Revue Bar! This might come as a surprise to you but it wouldn't do a thing for me.'

'Young GD type like you? I thought you lads were like hand grenades with the pins taken out?'

'Not this one, mate! Not at the moment anyway. I'll let you know when the first "stirrings" occur!'

'Fine, I'd be obliged if you would. It makes my job so much easier.'

The rest of the morning passed with me browsing over some files and it went on like that for another week. One morning the kindly 'adj' handed me his phone. It was Doug Rutherford.

'What's it like up there in the flesh-pots of Uxbridge, then?'

'Hilarious! I don't think I can stand the pace!'

'That sounds more like the old Mike Kendrick I once knew. Listen, get into your lounge suit and come up to Adastral. We'll have a few jars and a pub lunch. This afternoon, I want you to meet my boss. Now, don't worry! He's one of the best. Knows how to communicate and he's good with people.'

'What's he doing in Personnel, then?'

'I'll pretend I didn't hear that. Seriously though, Mike, you will like Wing-Co Lewis. He's a Welshman, come up the hard way. Ex apprentice, passed out top of his entry at Halton and awarded a scholarship to Cranwell. You know what that means!'

'I sure do. He'll probably finish off the hatchet- job that SASO began in Germany.'

'Think Mike! Think about everything SASO said to you, then come up and see my Wing-Co. Can you make it by one? I've a provisional booking for you to see him at two thirty.'

'See you outside "the buildings" at one, Doug. I've got nothing else better to do today, cheers!'

As I replaced the receiver, the adjutant turned to me.

'Looks as if things are happening. For what it's worth, I hope they sort things out for you. This might come as a surprise to you too, but I've always held your branch of the service in the highest esteem.'

'Wish I could say the same for the rest of your fraternity, Adj.'

'One rotten apple doesn't have to spoil the rest of the barrel and well you know it!'

When he said that I realised he knew a great deal more than he was prepared to say.

'OK. Point taken. I'm off to change now for Adastral. Ever wondered why we have to go into civilian dress each time we appear there?'

'You've still got a lot to learn, haven't you. Don't you know that civil servants get all inhibited at the sight of us? Most service establishments are infested with them these days.'

I thought that was rather an odd statement. Perhaps the old 'adj' had reasons for making it but I didn't pursue it.

Douglas Rutherford and I had a pleasant pub lunch. He wanted to know how Russ Tillis was getting on.

'Good pilot was Russ. He won the aerobatics trophy at the college and did a damn good tour with No. 1 Squadron. I would have given my right arm for that posting!'

'Yes, I remember now. One of the best display pilots in the service. I saw him at Farnborough once. Never mind, we can't all be the ace of the base!'

'Well, he's been brought down to earth now, Mike. Running around in ever decreasing circles until he disappears up his own arse, trying to keep up with the air marshals!'

'Oh, he's all right!'

'Russ or his air marshal?'

'Both of them. You told me over the phone to think about everything SASO had said. Well, I have. I quote, "depending upon subsequent enquiries here, you may be the subject of a Summary of Evidence. Failing that, the Air Secretary will decide what is to be done with you" – unquote.'

Doug finished off his pint.

'Come on, Mike. It's time for you to meet big Dai Lewis. If he can't sort you out nobody can!'

A rather attractive bar-maid collected our empty glasses, then asked Doug if there was anything else he wanted. Much to my surprise, Doug leaned over the counter.

'I'll think of something between now and 10.30 tonight, gorgeous.'

The girl giggled and I remember saying, 'Based on that performance, Squadron Leader, I reckon Russ Tillis will make chief of air staff before you do!'

'He'll make it anyway, whether I fell by the wayside or not! He's had the magic wand waved over his head. He'll get to the top "irrespective of performance in post" and I've seen that in print before now. Once the stamp of golden boy gets slapped on a chap's file, that's it!'

As we walked together down Northampton Row towards Adastral, I asked Doug about his own future.

'It will be three years' hard labour without remission for good behaviour up here. I'm supposed to have my pick of the postings after this. OC Bee-keepers at Kyrenia would be nice. Sue's always twittering away about Cyprus.'

'How is the lovely Susan? Well, I hope?'

'Yes, she's fine, thanks. Was asking about you the other day. Wanted to know if you were married yet. When I told her you weren't, she reminded me of your antics with the bridesmaids at our wedding!'

'Yes, those were the days. Leuchars in the fifties. It's an age ago now, isn't it?'

Back in Doug's office, we sat chatting about the old days for a while. I still had fifteen minutes to wait before my interview with Wing Commander Lewis. Doug mentioned his involvement in the Battle of Britain Association, purely on a correspondence level. He said that there was some talk of a film being made about it. Finding the aircraft for this would be a job. It would take ages. I suddenly had a thought.

'Where's the Air Historical Branch by the way?'

'What do you want to know that for?'

'I've been doing a spot of research on the Battle of Britain myself. There's a Luftwaffe war grave at home. Our vicar's very interested in it. I don't suppose it would be possible for me to have a look at some of the old combat reports?'

'Wait a minute. Let's consult the directory.'

Doug got up and took a booklet off the shelf. He thumbed through it.

'Yes, here it is. Head of section is a Mr Chekkitts. It must be an all civil service department.'

'Do you think you could use your vast powers of charm and persuasion on Mr Chekkitts? See if he will let me browse through reports for the 9 September, 1940?'

'When would you want to do that?'

'When Lewis has finished with me. I've got the rest of the

afternoon free.'

Doug dialled a number on his phone. After a few seconds he got through.

'Hello, Mr Chekkitts? We haven't met before but my name's Rutherford. I'm with the Air Secretary's Branch. Yes, that's right. I've been nominated to process the correspondence for the Battle of Britain Association. Have they? I didn't know that! Well, I was wondering if you could help me. I've got a Flight Lieutenant Kendrick with me today and he's doing a spot of research for us.'

Doug winked at me as he said that.

'If possible, he would like to read some of the old combat reports. Yes, I imagine they are. Our archives are in the same state, I'm afraid. Just the one day at present, 9 September, 1940. Yes, I can appreciate that, September would be the biggest batch you've got. Yes, I understand.'

There was a pause in the conversation and Doug rolled his eyes upwards and drummed his fingers on the desk.

'Yes, that would be fine. About an hour you say? I'll give Kendrick your room number. Many thanks Mr Chekkitts, good bye.'

Doug reached for his memo pad.

'He's got to get one of his minions to sort things out. Blow off the dust and untie the ribbons. Sounds a very pleasant chap actually!'

As Doug jotted down the floor and room number for me a very large gentleman entered the office. He looked like a professional rugby player. He had a wide forehead and alert blue eyes. He pointed a stubby finger at me.

'You Kendrick?'

Knowing this had to be Lewis, I stood up and said, 'Yes, sir.'

Doug remained seated. He'd seen the wing- co in action before. Lewis pointed his thumb towards the adjoining door.

'In you go then. It's a no-smoking zone in there, by the way.'

As I went into his torture chamber, this Torquemada of the Valleys went to the filing cabinet and removed a batch of papers. To my surprise he grinned.

'It's Mike Kendrick isn't it? I'm Dai Lewis. Take a pew.'

He offered me his hand and when I shook it nearly lost three fingers. When we were both seated he started.

'You wouldn't be the first young officer to get himself into a pickle, boyo, and I dare say you won't be the last – more's the pity! Among other things, I run the Humpty-Dumpty department around here. Like it says in the rhyme, we can never put all the pieces back together again. What we have to do is collect enough of them to do a patch-up job. One way or another, the bits we find have got to be put to some practical use. You have cost the tax payer a lot of money. Not only for your training but the experience you've acquired since then. Flying experience, I'm talking about now. We can't throw that away when we've got you for the next five years. If we did that, the Treasury would be after us. Looking through your 1369s I see your assessments as a pilot were consistently above the average. Group Captain Templewood doesn't think you're cut out for the V-force and neither do I. Not that you deserve it, but we're going to do you a favour by putting you in the Transport Force. Work hard there and in five years' time you could leave the service with enough route experience to interest some unsuspecting, long suffering airline! They may not be taking service pilots now but, the position will change as the wartime bulge of captains move into retirement. Any question so far?'

'Yes, sir. Aren't the airlines training their own pilots from scratch now at Hamble?'

'They are and no doubt they will do a good job. Despite that, there's no substitute for service training and I think some of the top civil management knows it!'

'Can I assume, sir, that charges are not being made against me for what happened in Germany?'

Lewis looked a bit belligerent and he leaned over his desk towards me.

'You can't assume a damn thing, boyo! You came to within a gnat's whisker of a general court's martial. Step out of line just once more and your services will be dispensed with long before your 38/16 point!'

Lewis was just being tough but I had the answer I wanted.

'Right then,' he continued. 'It's off to Manby next week for a full refresher course and multi- engine conversion. After that it's Britannia's at Lyneham. You're going to be busy between now and the next six months, believe me!'

I thought of asking Lewis about contacts with Düsseldorf but decided against it. Perhaps that side of things would be handled elsewhere. Lewis had done his wing commander act and sat back in his chair with just a hint of a smile.

'I knew your SASO when he was my first station commander. That was years ago when I flew Javelin night fighters. OK, so he was a strict disciplinarian but he was always fair, Mike. I don't think there are any real villains in your story. Just fallible human beings with all their weaknesses. The big trick is to weld them all together in such a way that we get a difficult job done. Now go on, get out of here before I change my mind!'

I stood up and said 'Thank you, sir. Good afternoon.' I was relieved he didn't offer to shake hands again. My fingers were still a bit numb. Out again in Doug's office I saw he had two coffees on his table.

'So now you know the diabolical plot, mate. Here, take a swig of this.'

I thanked him and enjoyed the coffee. Doug collected some papers together.

'When big Dai was playing Rugby for the RAF, they say he used to hurl himself at brick walls for practice.'

I said that I could believe that all right.

'I've worked for a lot worse than him in my time, I can tell you. He believes loyalty should be two-way traffic. Upwards and downwards. Here's your travel warrant for Manby, by the way. This is your course attachment authority and the posting notice for Lyneham will follow. You better wend your way up to see Chekkitts now, Mike. Mustn't keep civil servants waiting, especially when they're in a cooperative mood!'

'Thanks Doug. Thanks for everything!'

We shook hands and I left the office, walked down the corridor to the lift and glanced at the room number Doug had jotted down for me. I found Air Historical Branch on the fifth floor and tapped on the door. Mr Chekkitts bade me enter and I noticed in the corner of the room an empty desk with a pile of papers on it. They looked brown with age. Mr Chekkitts said he hoped I would find what I was looking for.

'You may not find it, though. An awful lot of engagements took place and not all those involved in the fighting got back to write about it. Some of the pilots just gave the bare facts verbally to their unit intelligence officers. The IOs had to do the writing for them!'

I thanked him for this and sat down at the desk. I felt what I was going to read would take my mind off my own troubles for a while. That's probably why I'd asked Doug Rutherford to arrange it. I noticed with another tinge of alarm a no-smoking sign in the office. Undaunted, I picked up the first batch of reports and started to read. The style and terminology was dated. Abbreviations all over the place. Written in a hurry no doubt. E.A. for enemy aircraft, Angels instead of Altitude, cloud amounts in tenths instead of eights, and so on. Most of the engagements were timed between 5.30 and 6pm. Those recording attacks on bombers I dismissed. Batch One revealed nothing so I picked up another pile. One report made me smile. It read: 'Attack E.A. 109, Poof! Time 1740. Maidstone area'. It was signed by a Polish pilot in a shaky hand. Then, the first reference to Me110s started to appear. These had been written by pilots operating out of Duxford. As far as I remembered that was 12 Group territory. Bennecker had referred to the first appearance of that group in the Battle. I felt I was getting warm. The report that really riveted my attention must have been written by an IO on behalf of the pilot.

'Time 1750. Croydon area. Formation of Me110s attacked. Outer E.A. of formation executed slow roll after hits observed. Broke off attacks as pursued by E.A. in rear.'

Although the pilot had signed the report his signature was indecipherable. I noticed the squadron number had been added in another hand, probably IO's. It was 310 Squadron. I carried on reading and began the last batch. One of these had been written by a pilot who claimed to have destroyed a Dornier.

'Time 1750. Croydon area. E.A.Do 17 attacked. Blew up. Narrowly missed by E.A.Me110. Inverted in dive. One parachute seen to deploy.'

I finished off reading those reports but nothing further caught my eye.

Folding them, I put them back in the original order and stood up. Mr Chekkitts looked up from his desk.

'Any luck?'

I thought for a second.

'Yes, I think so. Do you happen to have a list of squadrons that took part at this time, Mr Chekkitts?'

'Not in this office. Try next door. Miss Abbott keeps a small reference library there. Tell her I sent you.'

'Thanks very much, Mr Chekkitts. I'm most grateful to you.'

I left Chekkitt's office and tapped on the door next to his. A lady wearing glasses and twin-set opened the door. I introduced myself and explained the purpose of my visit. She looked a little flustered.

'Well, you better take a look on that shelf over there. Try Dempster and Wood's *Narrow Margin*. You might find what you're looking for.'

Miss Abbott was as good as her word. I found the book and in the indices at the back of it, a list of participating RAF squadrons by phases of the battle. No. 310 Squadron operated out of Duxford and although commanded by a British squadron leader at the time, the pilots were all Czechs. I turned to Miss Abbott and plucked up courage.

'I don't suppose you've anything on squadron histories, Miss Abbott?'

She said she hadn't and suggested I tried the main library on the ground floor. I thanked her and left.

When I arrived at the library I asked the lady there if she had anything on squadron histories. She looked up her own index and pointed to her left.

'Row E, under E432. If it's still there. Are you taking it out? I'm closing shortly.'

'No, I won't be doing that, thank you. Just want a quick glance at it to take a reference.'

I turned and walked down Row E. Checking the numbers, I was pleased to find the book. Sitting on a nearby chair I flicked through the pages and found 310 Squadron. I read it quickly and was surprised at the names of Czech pilots mentioned. Hess, Bergmann, Schnabel, etc. They all sounded like Germans! My knowledge of Czech history was limited to say the least. I knew about the Sudetenland but didn't realise the full significance of it.

'What an irony,' I thought. 'Neumann shot down and killed by a Czech pilot whose ancestors probably hailed from Germany!'

I closed the book and replaced it on the shelf. I thanked the librarian on my way out and received a curt nod.

On my way back to Uxbridge on the Underground, I thought about those combat reports.

'Same day, same time, same place. That Me110 must have been Neumann's in the first report. It was the second one that posed the problem. If the Messerschmitt referred to in that was the same, then somebody got out of it after all!'

There was no question in my mind of imparting this information to Paul Channing. He would only go off at another tangent. Like a lot of other things, I would have to keep that to myself.

At Uxbridge I called in to see the adjutant the next day. I showed him my attachment authority to Manby and told him about the Lyneham posting. He was genuinely pleased.

'You'll like Wiltshire. I'm a moonraker myself. Born and bred in Chippenham. The beer's good and the girls buxom!'

I tried to look disinterested.

'You've either got a poor opinion of pilots, Adj, or you're just obsessed with sex!'

He smiled.

'Don't forget to sign out when you go. Pay your mess bill too, please. They don't like sending them on for small amounts. All the best and happy landings!'

'So long, Adj,' I said. 'Enjoy your retirement. Might bump into you in Chippenham one day, I wouldn't wonder!'

I left his office and went back to my room in the mess. That evening I wrote the first of two letters that had been on my mind since leaving Germany.

17

I still had a couple of days in hand before my course started and now that the risk of a court martial had gone – decided to go home. My parents were surprised to see me and I told them all about the dramas in Rheindahlen. They were sympathetic enough but I could see they thought I had made an awful botch of things.

'Paul Channing is back home again now, dear,' said my mother. 'Why don't you pop over and see him? They got those two young muggers who attacked him, you know.'

My father nodded and looked angry.

'Absolute scandal, that. I hope they get a good long stretch for GBH, the pair of them. As for Squires, they can put him down and throw away the key.'

'Squires? What did he have to do with it?' I asked in amazement.

'You better talk to Paul' said my mother. 'It's a long story, dear, and not a pretty one. You ought to hear it from him I think.'

After tea I rang the Channings and they were equally surprised at my sudden homecoming. I was invited over that evening and we sat down together in their lounge. When I told them what had happened in Germany, Heather frowned.

'Well, that was bloody silly, wasn't it? You might have had some satisfaction at the time telling that old pig his fortune but they'll never forgive you for it, Mike!'

Paul looked annoyed at Heather.

'You think he doesn't know that? He doesn't need us to rub it in! I'm terribly sorry to hear what's happened, especially about Ewalt. In a round about way, I feel partially responsible. If it hadn't been for all this German business things might have been different!'

'No they wouldn't, Paul. I would still have felt the same way about Dieter Ewalt. Thanks all the same. What's all this I hear about Squires and the muggers?'

Heather sat back in her chair, resigned to hearing the whole story for the umpteenth time. Paul offered his wife another drink to deaden the pain but she declined. He offered me a refill which I accepted and pouring a generous measure for himself, he told me what had happened in Tallingwood since my last leave.

'It was DC Barber who really solved it. He never liked Squires and started a lot of enquiries about him. Among the many facts to emerge was that Squires had been captured at Anzio in 1944. He had a rough time until he was liberated in Germany at the end of the war. While he was in the bag his younger sister was killed by a VI flying bomb in Croydon High Street. That news, coupled to all his experiences as a POW, led to a long-term hatred of everything German.'

I interrupted Paul at this point with a reminder that Squires had supported the Rev. Latimer in his plans to trace the Neumann relatives.

'That was just a blind – a cover for what he was really thinking and planning to do. Before being shipped out to North Africa in '42, Squires had served in France with the British Expeditionary Force. He was a bofors gunner and was lucky to be evacuated from Dunkirk. He was stationed at Kenley during the Battle of Britain and went through the whole thing as part of the airfield defences. One night some weeks ago, there was a brawl at the Red Lion involving some of the local lads and a couple of visitors. The ensuing rough-house was certainly started by the two strangers but our lads finished it. Several arrests were made when the police arrived and they were charged at Tallingwood Station. Before being put into the cells for the night, personal effects were confiscated and it was these that Barber took an interest in the following morning. One of the 'visitors' had a wallet and would you believe, it contained a credit card which didn't belong to him!'

'I suppose it was yours!'

'Got it in one! I'd cancelled it with the bank weeks before, shortly after being laid out in the Grove. Anyway, Barber spent a long time questioning "chummy" with the wallet and, later that morning was joined by Truscott. It didn't take long for him to get a confession out of the visiting thugs! One of them said he had visited his uncle in Tallingwood the day before to collect some money. When both villains were told they would face additional charges and be identified, they sang like a couple of canaries. Uncle, of course, was Albert Squires. He had paid them for the job they did on my tyres in addition to the assault-course in the Grove.'

'Who told you all this, Paul?' I asked that as it seemed a little uncharacteristic of the police.

'Well, they had to in the end. Truscott came round that evening and told me. Both he and Barber had paid a visit to uncle Albert and given him a good grilling. After some initial resistance, Squires admitted organizing the whole thing. He said his nephew was putting the screws on him for more money – trying to blacken his nephew's case even further, if he could!'

'What about motives in Squire's case, Paul? Didn't Truscott say anything about that?' I thought that was worth asking.

'There must have been plenty. Squires told Truscott how he had seen wounded British POWs machine-gunned to death by Waffen SS troops outside Anzio. Barber's revelations about the sister's death in Croydon clinched it. Squires regards the Germans as vermin.'

'What about 1940? Do you think Squires knew anything about the Plover's Green case?'

Heather sighed as I put that question to Paul.

'He probably did, being in the area at the time. Truscott wouldn't have raised that with him, of course. I went to see Squires myself last week. He's still in custody awaiting trial with the other two. I didn't get very far with him as you can imagine. He called me a lot of rude names when I mentioned the Plover's Green enquiries.'

'Will you have to give evidence at the trial?' I asked.

'I don't see how it can be avoided. The police won't take too kindly to any references to Plover's Green in court, though.'

'No, I don't suppose they would. Prosecuting counsel will probably refer to "general enquiries" about the war which Squires found offensive.'

Heather had heard enough and got up to make coffee in the kitchen. When she had gone, Paul continued.

'I haven't told you the best bit yet. Two days ago I had a caller at the *Times* office who said his name was Langford. I took that with a pinch of salt, together with his Home Office credentials. I was treated to a long lecture on the public interest and reminded about Government D Notices. He didn't like what I had been doing here in Tallingwood and said that now a court case was brewing I should be very "circumspect" – as he put it!'

I was surprised to hear this and wanted to know more.

'What was your reaction to that? Did you tell him what you thought happened here in 1940?'

'I did indeed and he just sat there stony-faced and trotted out the party line about there being no evidence in support of rumours of that kind.'

'Fair enough, Paul, but suppressing wild rumours would be part of his job, particularly if they were going to be aired in court. You can't blame him for that.'

'So you still don't think it ever happened, Mike?'

'I haven't told you this before Paul but while you were in hospital, the police put me on to somebody who was actually there at Vernon Road shortly after the crash. Neumann was identified all right, there was no doubt about it.'

Paul looked rather annoyed.

'Why didn't you tell me about that at the time?'

'I didn't think you were well enough for one thing and I wanted to get your mind off it for another.'

'All right, Mike, but that still doesn't explain what happened to the second member of that crew. Surely that must have occurred to you?'

'Maybe it did but it's all very inconclusive. Bennecker didn't think Baumbach could have abandoned that aircraft, given the circumstances.'

'He might have been wrong, Mike, he wasn't in the bloody thing! Are "G" forces variable in a spiral dive? You're the Birdman around here, put your thinking cap on!'

I could have taken offence at that challenge but I didn't. I knew full well what Paul was getting at.

'That spiral could have flattened out at some stage. All aircraft have a natural stability about the lateral axis. Somewhere between 18,000 feet and bale-out it could have happened, I suppose. That would have given Baumbach his chance. It's pure speculation on my part and nothing more.'

Paul thought for a moment and continued on another track.

'Would it have been possible for absolutely nothing to have been found of Baumbach had he remained on board to the end?'

'No. I don't think so. There would have been something there.'

'Well, at least it's got you thinking about it, Mike.'

Heather re-entered the lounge at this point with the coffee cups.

'What's he supposed to be thinking about now?' she asked.

'Your appearance in court or what's been happening to us as a family!'

Paul didn't look at all pleased with his wife's comments and quickly finished off the remains of his drink. Heather was going to give me a piece of her mind.

'I want to leave Tallingwood. As a result of all this unpleasantness, you can imagine what it has been like for us. When my children came home from school one day and asked me what a "Kraut-lover" was, that was it! When it gets to that level I want out of here, no matter what the cost. I know it's easier said than done with Paul's job, the sale of the house and finding somewhere else to settle. I've had all I can stand of it, Mike.'

I could see her point of view well enough. The victimization of their children was appalling – there was no denying that. Nevertheless, for Paul's sake I offered a crumb of comfort.

'I wouldn't let the lunatic fringe get the better of you, Heather. We all know about the mindless cruelties of the playground. My bet is the whole thing will blow over in time, in fact I'm sure it will.'

Heather looked doubtful but I could see Paul agreed with me.

'Yes, I think it will too. The little horrors will soon find something else to occupy their minds. I'm not going to be driven out of Tallingwood for that. Tell me Mike, what's going to happen to you now?'

Paul looked sympathetic as he asked that.

'I'll be leaving the service at thirty-eight and hopefully finding a slot in civil aviation. I've got a great deal to learn before that happens and I'm going to be especially busy in the coming months. There's plenty of unfinished business in Germany too but I can't attend to any of it yet!'

Heather nodded and gave a faint smile.

'Wasn't there some talk of a visit by the Germans to the war grave, Mike? A sister, I believe you said. Would that be some of the unfinished business?'

'I told them to get in touch with Latimer. They've got his address so the rest is up to them. When I spoke of unfinished business, I was thinking of Dieter Ewalt's widow.'

'Oh, I see' said Heather. 'Sorry if I got the wrong end of the stick.'

She wasn't sorry at all and I could see it written all over her face. Paul offered me another drink but I turned it down. We had covered a lot of ground that evening and I felt it was time to go. Perhaps I did feel a tinge of guilt at not telling Paul what I had read in those combat reports. Even if there was a strong likelihood of that parachute deployment being Baumbach's, there was still a lack of concrete evidence to prove it. I would only be speculating again if I told Paul of my suspicions, namely that the authorities, knowing full well what happened at Plover's Green, took the body right out of the area and buried it elsewhere. Somewhere between Maidstone and Walton-on-Thames, perhaps. Paul was looking tired anyway and I didn't want him dwelling on the case, if it could be avoided. As we stood at the doorway on my departure, I wished Paul good luck at the forthcoming trial and we promised to keep in touch.

As I drove home that night, I wondered what Padre Latimer must have thought about the arrest of Albert Squires, his so-called ally! It was a bad business all right and all I wanted to do then was spend a quiet time with my parents on the morrow before departing to Manby. At least I would be flying again and that was something to look forward to.

18

That first letter I wrote was to Lotte. I tried to find the right words and failed miserably. It was much the same when I tried to convey my thoughts and feelings to Inge. Putting Manby as my address, I had some vague hopes of a reply within a month or so. As it happened, Lotte did answer towards the end of my course. I remember reading that letter time and time again. It was the most heart-rending thing I'd ever read in my life and I prefer to keep the contents of it private even now, after all these years. Subsequent letters I received from Lotte showed she and her daughters were slowly getting back to life again, and in every letter, she asked when I was coming to Germany. She had taken Heidi and Helga back to her parents home in Lower Saxony. A place called Verden which I'd never heard of. Her father was a retired doctor and her mother was not too well. Lotte had taken over the running of the large rambling house and put all her energies into work. In one of her earlier letters she said she had heard that Inge Weber had gone to America on business and wanted to know if I had heard from her. I hadn't then and I still hadn't, months after the letter I wrote from Manby.

I did much the same as Lotte. Sank everything I had into my work. Although the Britannia was a handful in the early days, I was determined to master it. The work was interesting, so unlike anything I had done before. I spent plenty of time in the simulator and grabbed every manual I could lay my hands on. When the other co-pilots were relaxing, particularly down the routes, I studied and watched every move the experienced captains made. I was acquiring a reputation on the squadron for being too serious by half. The CO had me in one day and although satisfied with the training officer's reports, he made the following observations.

'Try and mix a little more with your brother officers,

173

Kendrick! They get a bit restive flying with you. It's all work and no play, isn't it? You make some of my captains feel uncomfortable too. They're not complaining, don't get that idea. They just wish you would make the odd minor mistake now and then. It would give them something to write about!'

I gave that some thought and realised the CO knew nothing of my fall from grace at Rheindahlen. If he had known, it would have explained everything. I was grateful P.2. and the Air Sec's boys had tidied up my documents. They had given me a break and the chance to make a fresh start. The CO concluded with these comments:

'It's going to be at least another six months before your next "Cat" ride. You've got more hours to clock up before we can even consider a captain's course for you. If your ambition in life is to get into the left-hand seat in record time, then understand it's going to depend upon experience. There's a West-about World trainer scheduled for the end of the month and I'm putting you on it. That's where the real experience lies!'

I thanked the CO for that and left his office.

Dave Osmond was one of our flight commanders. A tall, slim, prematurely grey squadron leader. He was a fine pilot, liked and respected by everyone. One morning shortly after the interview with the CO, Dave invited me into his office for a chat.

'When did you last take leave, Mike?'

'Not for a few months.'

'Five months in fact and that's far too long to go without a break.'

'The CO's putting me on a West-about this month and I don't want to miss it.'

'You could still get ten days off before that. Get away from here and put work behind you. Your home's in Surrey isn't it? Not far to travel from here?'

'Are you trying to get rid of me, sir?'

'For ten days I am. One of my jobs here is to keep a fatherly eye on co-pilots. I can't do that if I don't know what makes them tick. There's something about you, Mike. I don't know what it is yet but I've got to try and find out.'

I must have looked uncomfortable at that.

'Not another soul- searching inquisition!' I thought to

myself.

Dave produced the cigarettes. I took one and waited for the next bit.

'Most of us here have been in the Transport Force for a long time. Too long, some say! That means we don't know the chaps in other commands all that well. You had two tours on Hunters didn't you?'

I nodded.

Dave drew on his cigarette.

'What happened after that?'

'Did a spot of test flying at a maintenance unit. Thought of going to CFS but decided against it. I'd been warned about Training Command. They said it was a one-way ticket to years of sweating over a hot Bloggs!'

Dave grinned.

'What were you doing in Germany, Mike?'

'The dreaded ground-tour syndrome caught up with me. Some sadist thought I needed it. I was pushing thirty then, anyway. Had to make room for the kiddiwinks!'

'What were you doing out there in RAFG?'

'Org and admin. A fate worse than death as the Virgin cried.'

Dave laughed and shook his head.

'Oh dear! Was that where you came unstuck?'

'I hated it. The other GD lads did too. Rheindahlen was bursting at the seams with top brass. You can imagine what our lives were like!'

Dave nodded.

'Upset anybody there, did you?'

'Don't think my group captain was all that impressed!'

'Uh-huh! Well, that answers some of the questions. You lead a pretty quiet social life, don't you. We don't see you in the bar very much. As a bachelor, you must have an interest in the normal pursuits?'

He said that with a grin.

'If I did, I wouldn't do it here.'

'So the unattached ladies tell me. You're something of a challenge to them.'

'I hope you're not suggesting anything sinister.' I said that with a forced smile.

'If I thought you were a fairy, Mike, I'd say so. OK, enough of the agony aunt. Take that spot of leave. I'll re-arrange the crew lists with Ops. Thank you for filling in the gaps by the way. At least I know something about you now.'

I stubbed the cigarette out in Dave's ash tray.

'I'll fill in a leave pass and drop it in to your office for signature this afternoon, sir.'

Back in the mess that night I thought about my leave. Germany was where I ought to go. I imagined how it would be if I did. Verden, Lower Saxony would be the first call. I'd run to Lotte and her little ones. There would be tears all round as I hugged them. I wasn't sure I was ready for that yet and even less sure that Lotte was.

Then Inge. She was always in my thoughts. Not one word from her in all this time. Nothing from the provost marshal's office either. I thought someone there might have enquired if I'd made contact again. The fact they hadn't indicated no change in the situation and I wondered again whether my letter was ever delivered to her. No, I wouldn't go to Germany this time. It was too soon for that. I'd go home to Tallingwood. Relax with my parents and look up the Channings. Paul must have given me up for lost. I hadn't written since I left Rheindahlen.

I collected my leave pass the next morning and with a few things packed in a case, drove my car out of the main gates of Lyneham.

It was a fine May morning and the drive home was pleasant. Mother had lunch ready when I arrived and she said I looked tired and made the usual rumbling noises about losing weight.

'What on earth are they doing to you at Lyneham, dear? Aren't they feeding you properly?'

'They feed those who want it very well, Mum. I just haven't got the appetite these days, that's all. How's Dad?'

'He's on the golf course today. Your father eats like a horse, I'm glad to say. Retirement suits him. He's been doing some part-time accountancy work for a law firm which keeps him from getting under my feet all day. Your Aunt Molly wishes your Uncle Ben would do the same. Ben's such an old fuss-pot! He drives poor Molly to distraction at times!'

I smiled at that.

'Yes, Uncle Ben led such an active life in Customs and Excise. He really ought to find some outlets for his energies.'

Mother looked a bit doubtful.

'Well, at least he's not chasing the barmaids like that dreadful old roué down the road. He ought to be ashamed of himself at his age!'

'Who is that, may I ask?'

'Norah Linton's husband. Retired last year and spends all his time trying to date the dolly birds behind the bar at the Red Lion.'

'Life in the old dog yet! Either that or it's the male menopause.'

'Poor Norah. I feel so sorry for her! Given that old devil the best years of her life and now this. It's scandalous. Met any nice girls at Lyneham yet, dear?'

Mother was about to embark on her usual theme of conversation.

'Oh yes, loads of them. We have orgies every week end in the mess. I can't keep up with it. Perhaps that's why I'm looking tired and thin!'

Mother looked shocked.

'I know it's one of your Air Force jokes Michael but you know I don't like that sort of humour. Keep that for your father when he gets in.'

'Sorry, Mum, I'll behave during the rest of my leave – promise. Any news of Angela?'

Mother frowned.

'You don't write to her often enough, you know. She and Bill have had their fair share of quarrels. Your sister wants to start a family and Bill wants to wait.'

'That may be on financial grounds, Mum. Teaching's not the best paid job, is it?'

'Stuff and nonsense! He's either being selfish or avoiding the responsibility!'

I didn't want to get embroiled in an argument about that so changed the subject.

'Seen anything of the Channings lately?'

'I bumped into Heather about a month ago. She was collecting a prescription from the chemist in the High Street. Paul has been off work again with headaches. That dreadful mugging has left its mark on him. All that time ago too. Heather looked washed out but did ask how you were. I think they're rather peeved you haven't kept in touch, dear.'

'I'll ring them tonight and treat them out to dinner next week. Sounds as if it would do them good!'

Mother started to clear the plates off the lunch table.

'That would be nice, dear. Can't you find someone to make up a foursome?'

'Milly Watkins, she ought to be safe enough!'

'Who is she, may I ask?'

'Paul's secretary at the *Times* office. Sweet fifty-five and never been kissed!'

'Michael!'

There was a warning note in Mother's voice even if she did smile. There was a thump in the hall. My father had come in and dumped his golf clubs.

'Hello Mike! You're looking well!'

My mother snorted and took the plates into the kitchen.

'Hello Dad. Good round of golf?'

He sat down in his favourite chair.

'Not bad, thanks. Plenty of good exercise. How are things at Lyneham? Keeping you busy are they? Haven't had much leave, have you!'

I didn't tell him that was by choice.

'It's one of the busiest stations in the country, Dad. I'm off on a round the world trip at the end of the month.'

I described the route to him and he listened intently.

'How lucky you are,' he said finally. 'What a wonderful life! I can think of a lot of chaps who would give anything to be in your shoes!'

He lit his pipe and I waited until Vesuvius stopped erupting.

'You were in the Home Guard, weren't you, Dad?'

'That's right. Not until 1942 though. Why do you ask?'

'Just wondered if you knew Paul's father. He was in it right early on.'

'Channing the solicitor?'

'That's him. He was in the LDV before it became the Home Guard.'

'It's a long time ago now. He died in the fifties, didn't he?'

'Yes. It was all very sudden. Heart trouble I believe. It shook the family.'

'I'm sure it did. Channing, yes I do remember him now. Tall chap with a dry sense of humour. They wanted him as platoon sergeant but he turned it down.'

'Any idea why?'

'Something about the extra hours of training it would involve. He was running that law practice single-handed during the war. The younger chaps had all joined up!'

I wondered how to broach the next subject with my father.

'He told his wife on the quiet about an incident at Plover's Green. Young Paul did a spot of eavesdropping. Very naughty, of course.'

My father had to re-light his pipe. When he had finished the ignition sequence he looked up.

'He never mentioned it to me or anyone else. When was the incident?'

'At the height of the Blitz. September 1940. German parachute down at Plover's.'

'No. That was two years before I joined the Home Guard. Ancient history by then.'

'Well, it's certainly ancient history by now!'

'What made you bring it up then?'

'The vicar at Angela's wedding started it all. There's a German war grave at St Michael's. He asked me to try and find any relatives still living in Germany. I had thought there may have been a connection between the grave and the Plover's parachute story.'

'Why should the vicar be interested in all that?'

'I don't really know, Dad. He just said that nobody from Germany had ever visited the grave since the war. Perhaps he thought the relatives were unaware of its location. That sort of thing did happen sometimes.'

'Did you find anybody?'

'Eventually, yes. It took a long time. We had a lot of help from the Germans.'

'I hope they were suitably impressed!'

'I like to think they were. At least we made the effort.'

My father was clearly bored by this topic and asked me what plans I had for my leave.

'I shall just look up some old friends, I think. Have a nice lazy time. Want any help in the garden?'

He brightened up at this and said he was losing the battle with the weeds, as usual. If the good weather continued he would be delighted to see me in action, any time.

That evening I rang the Channings but there was no reply. I

rang again next morning with the same result. Beginning to feel uneasy, I decided to call in at the *Times* office.

Sitting at the breakfast table with my mother, I felt an irritation in my right eye and Mother said it was inflamed. In her opinion, and she was often right re minor ills, it was conjunctivitus. She recommended Brolene eye drops for it and as I was going into the High Street that morning, suggested I called in at the chemist. By the time I had changed after breakfast the eye started to water. If there was an infection there, the sooner medication was applied the better.

Mother asked me what time I wanted lunch.

'After a breakfast like that, Mum, I could skip lunch. I've got a lot to do and plenty of people to see. An evening meal would be fine for me.'

Mother shook her head sadly.

'No wonder you're losing weight, dear. You really must look after yourself. You're smoking too much as well. It was like the Blackwall Tunnel in here last night. You and your father's pipe! I'll be the next one to get conjunctivitus!'

I gave her a peck on the cheek and a quick hug.

'See you later, Mum. Tell Dad I'll do the weeds tomorrow.'

It was another nice day. Dry and sunny. I admired the neat, well kept front gardens everywhere.

It took me fifteen minutes to get to the centre of Tallingwood. The old place hadn't changed much. Turning into the High Street, I looked into a few shop windows on my way to the *Times* office. I walked in and heard a typewriter in action behind the office doors. I knocked and waited. The typing continued so I knocked again.

'Yes!' snapped the unmistakable voice of Milly Watkins.

I opened the door and gave what I hoped was an engaging smile.

'Sorry to bother you but I was wondering if Paul Channing was in? My name is Kendrick. I'm an old friend of his.'

Milly looked suspicious.

'Well, he's not here. He's taken the family on holiday.'

'May I ask when he's due back?'

'They've gone to Majorca for two weeks. They left on Saturday.'

'I see. How is he, by the way?'

'Mr Channing was advised by his doctor to take this

180

holiday. We've all been very worried about him for some time.'

'Yes. I expect you have. That was a bad business last year. The mugging, surgery and all the rest. I personally felt he went back to work too soon.'

'You weren't the only one,' sniffed Milly.

'Would you be so kind as to tell Mr Channing I called? I haven't been able to contact him for some time. I'm in the services and have to travel a lot. I could write, of course, but a personal meeting would have been so much better.'

'When are you likely to be in Tallingwood again?' asked Milly.

'Not until the autumn. It's a question of getting leave. Next time I'll write well in advance. I hope Mr Channing enjoys his holiday and returns refreshed!'

'So do I,' said Milly. 'What was your name again?'

'Kendrick. Michael Kendrick.'

She gave a curt nod and continued her typing. I had heard about Milly Watkins and realised why she annoyed Paul.

As I walked out of the *Times* office I thought about all the crosses he had to bear. I could think of two for a start – both female! Across the High Street, opposite the *Times* office I spotted Layton's the florist. They had a fine selection of flowers in their window and another thought came to mind.

My eye was running again and I had to dab it with my handkerchief. Getting my priorities right, I went into Boots and bought the Brolene. I ought to have applied the drops straight away but there was nowhere for me to do this. I thought about those flowers again and went into Laytons. They made up a bunch for me and I started the long walk to the parish church.

When I got there it seemed only fitting and proper for me to call in at the vicarage. I hadn't seen Padre Latimer since that leave I took from Rheindahlen. That seemed such a long time ago. The hinges on the vicarage gates could have done with some lubrication. They squeaked badly. I walked up the garden path and knocked on the door. I had to wait awhile before it was opened. A plump, motherly woman opened it and I recognised her immediately.

'Hello Mrs Woodford. Rememeber me? I'm Michael Kendrick. You taught Sunday school when I was knee high to a grass-hopper!'

She beamed.

'My, haven't you changed, Michael! We haven't seen you for a long time. What brings you here? What a lovely bunch of flowers.'

I knew that Mrs Woodford was the vicar's house-keeper and had been for some years.

'Is the vicar in by any chance? He asked me to do a job for him.'

'No dear. He's gone to Canterbury for the Synod. He's been wanting to do that for ages. He was so thrilled when his turn came, bless him! What was the job he asked you to do? You're in the Air Force aren't you?'

'That's right, Mrs Woodford. It was about the German war grave.'

'Goodness, gracious! He told me about that. They were only here a few weeks ago!'

'They?'

'Yes. A Mr and Mrs Benner, I think.'

'Bennecker?'

'Yes. That was the name. Such a nice couple. They spoke perfect English, both of them. It was Mrs Bennecker's brother that was buried here. The vicar had such a long chat with them. Mrs Bennecker was so nice. She complimented me on the cream tea and I knew the vicar was pleased. They had flowers with them too and they spent quite a time here. The vicar had to show them where the graves were. Mrs Bennecker wanted to lay some flowers on another grave, apart from her brother's.'

I swallowed hard at that.

'Did the vicar tell you about the other grave, Mrs Wood-ford?'

'Yes, he did. It was the family of four. A mother and her three sons. I can't remember the names now. The vicar told me about it afterwards.'

'Thank you, Mrs Woodford. I'm glad it all worked out in the end. Please give my regards to the vicar. If you will excuse me, I've got some flowers of my own to lay.'

She smiled again as I turned to leave.

'If you want a cup of tea afterwards, I'll put the kettle on. It's no trouble at all. Lovely to see you again, Michael.'

I thanked her and started to walk towards the churchyard.

When I arrived at the Lindsays' grave there were a few flowers worthy of the name still left. I removed the withered ones and replaced them from the bunch I had brought with me. I stood looking down at my handiwork for a moment and then glanced over to the left. To my surprise, Kurt Neumann's grave was still there. It ought to have been moved to Cannock Chase by then. I walked slowly towards that shabby wooden cross by the wall and knew what I had to do. I must have had at least a dozen flowers left over and as I neared Neumann's grave I saw much the same thing I had seen on the Lindsays' grave. A flower holder with a lot of faded blooms. I replaced them with what I had left. I must have stood there for quite a while. It was so very quiet there that day. I remembered thinking to myself then, 'What a shambles! What an utter shambles war is!'

I turned away in the end and started to walk out of the churchyard. To say that my heart was full would be the understatement of all time. It wasn't only the futility and waste of war or Dieter's death. It wasn't the loss of Inge either and that was bad enough. It wasn't only a chosen career in ruins, Paul Channing's ordeal or Lotte's agony. It was more than just that. If my left eye started watering then, it was for the whole of humanity.

The sun was very bright and as I strolled along the path, the sunlight flickered between the ash and elm trees in a psychedelic effect on my right eye. At the end of the path, two figures approached bearing flowers. A woman and a child. As we passed one another the child, a little girl, stared up at me and said in a piping voice:

'Mummy, what's that man crying for?'

'Hush dear,' said her mother and glanced over her left shoulder to watch me pass through those covered gates for the last time.

EPILOGUE

In 1985 a man in Luton was sifting through the personal effects of his father who had just died. Among the many small items he discovered what appeared to be a pair of identity discs. Remembering his father had been a soldier in World War II, he did not attach much importance to his find.

Showing the discs to a friend later, he was surprised to be told that they were German in origin. The friend explained the significance of the indentations on the discs which apparently belonged to an Unter- Offizier R.Baumbach. The man from Luton was mystified. He had no idea why his father should have retained these items as souvenirs. He was aware that his father had served on an Ack-Ack site in Surrey during the Battle of Britain but no mention was ever made as to how the discs were acquired. Perhaps like someone in Tallingwood, the man's father had tried to forget and failed.

About the people in this story

A few months after the events described in the last chapter of Kendrick's narrative, he went to Germany on leave. That reunion with Lotte Ewalt and her daughters was tearful, yes, but it was also a joyous one in the days that followed. He was a frequent visitor to Lower Saxony and this continued through out the remainder of his time in the RAF.

After sixteen years service, at the age of thirty-eight, Kendrick left the Royal Air Force and entered the world of civil aviation. This was a new life for him and the beginning of a long uphill struggle to the top of his profession.

Lotte Ewalt was to receive two proposals of marriage in the

184

early years of her widowhood, neither of which she accepted. As the years passed, her eldest daughter, Heidi, became a nurse and married a young doctor. They were to have two sons, christened Dieter and Michael.

Lotte's younger daughter, Helga, read modern languages at university and, upon graduation, entered Lufthansa as a stewardess.

By the early 1980s, Kendrick was a Boeing 747 captain on the Atlantic run. His company would occasionally fly other airline's cabin staff on a reciprocol arrangement. Lufthansa had requested by telex that two of their stewardesses be conveyed back to London from New York. Helga Ewalt was one of them.

As she and the other German girl boarded the great Jumbo Jet, she knew who the captain was and remembered a promise he had made to her when she was a little girl: 'If you're very good, I'll take you up in my aeroplane one day and we'll soar above the clouds together – you and I.'

This was the first occasion Helga had ever flown with Kendrick, which was rather surprising. He had been her stepfather for some time.

The West German counter-espionage authorities had continued their watch on Inge Bennecker, as she then was, until a decision was eventually taken. This was influenced by surveillance, interviews and finally on defectors' reports. Inge's meeting with Richter in Berlin was assessed as a coincidence. Her file in Bonn was duly annotated and 'put away.'

The Benneckers left Germany in 1970. Inge had been offered another highly-paid post in New York, which she accepted. She and Hugo became naturalized US citizens some years later and have not been heard of since.

The American officers in this story, Glen Hudson and Joe Skipton, knew each other well. This, in view of their joint NATO exchange status and, both of them made a point of keeping in touch with Lotte Ewalt after Dieter's death. Two years after that tragic event, Glen Hudson was able to introduce Joe Skipton to Kendrick at a NATO Reunion dinner in London. They had a lot to talk about. Both Skipton and Hudson retired as colonels from the USAF and, in later years whenever Kendrick had the chance, he would contact them during his duty visits to the United States. Those friendships were thus forged the hard way and nothing would ever sever them.

Paul Channing recovered his health gradually and he and his wife Heather still live in Tallingwood to this day. Paul gave up editing the *Times* when his first novel was published in 1975. He has made a comfortable living under a nom de plume ever since.

Both Rutherford and Tillis retired as air marshals, as Kendrick had predicted. Rutherford's son Christopher saw action in the Falklands conflict as a Harrier pilot.

'Per Adua ad Astra.'